DUMBNESS IS A DISH BEST SERVED COLD

THINK YOU CAN HANDLE
JAMIE KELLY'S FIRST YEAR OF DIARIES?

AND DON'T MISS . . .

Jim Benton's Tales from Mackerel Middle School

DEAR DUMB DIARY,

DUMBNESS IS A DISH BEST SERVED COLD

BY JAMIE KELLY

SCHOLASTIC INC.

All rights reserved. Published by Scholastic Inc., *Publishers since 1920.* SCHOLASTIC and associated logos are trademarks and/or registered trademarks of Scholastic Inc. DEAR DUMB DIARY is a registered trademark of Jim Benton.

Library of Congress Cataloging-in-Publication Data available

ISBN 978-0-545-93228-8

10 9 8 7 6 5 4 3 2 1   16 17 18 19 20
Printed in the U.S.A.   88
First printing, July 2016
Page design by Yaffa Jaskoll

For Shea, Ella, and Elaina.

Thanks to Kristen LeClerc, Shannon Penney,
Abby McAden, Sarah Evans, Yaffa Jaskoll,
and Emily Rader.

DUMBNESS IS A DISH BEST SERVED COLD

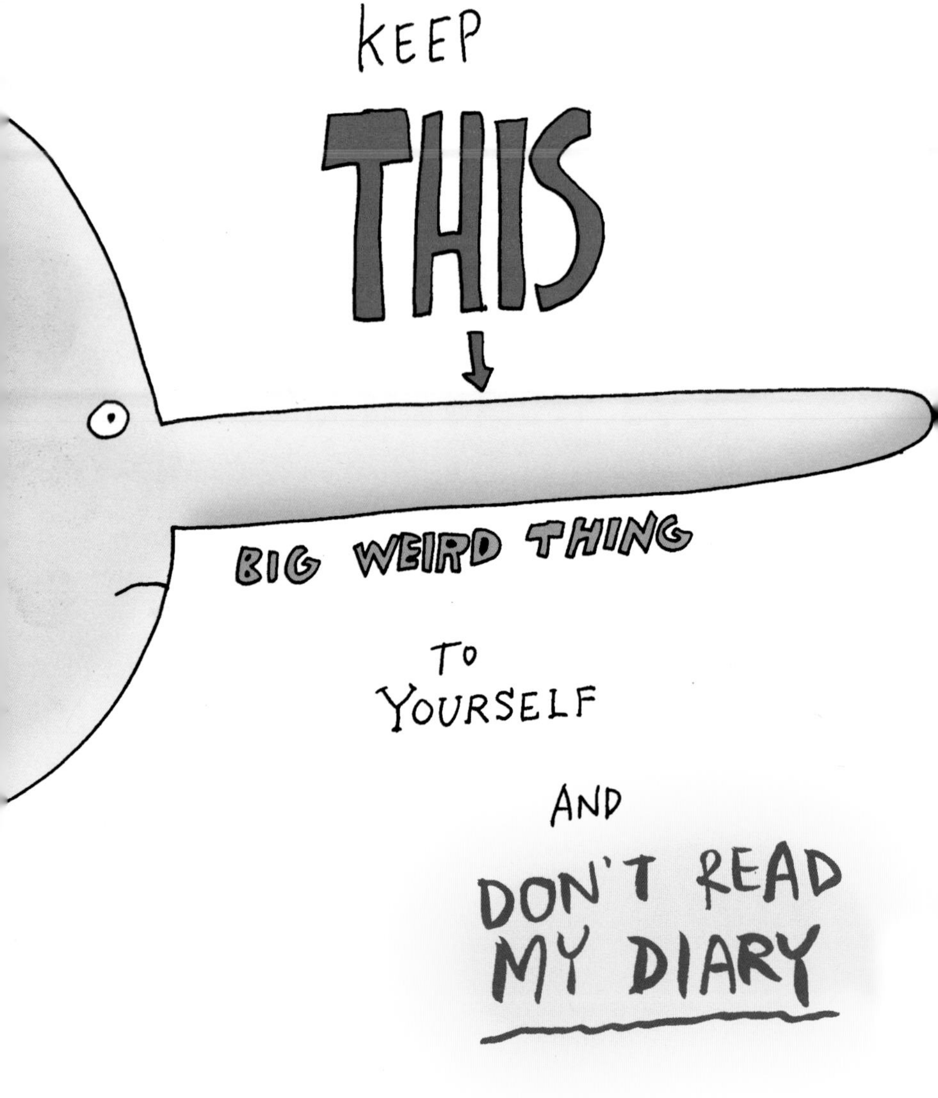
KEEP
THIS
BIG WEIRD THING
TO YOURSELF
AND
DON'T READ MY DIARY

Doctors say that we have to get our MINIMUM DAILY REQUIREMENT OF PRIVACY...

WHICH IS

A
TON
OF
PRIVACY

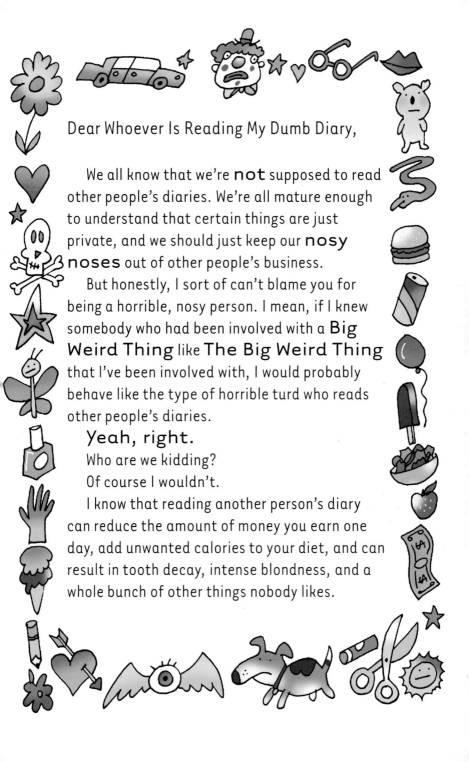

Dear Whoever Is Reading My Dumb Diary,

We all know that we're **not** supposed to read other people's diaries. We're all mature enough to understand that certain things are just private, and we should just keep our **nosy noses** out of other people's business.

But honestly, I sort of can't blame you for being a horrible, nosy person. I mean, if I knew somebody who had been involved with a **Big Weird Thing** like **The Big Weird Thing** that I've been involved with, I would probably behave like the type of horrible turd who reads other people's diaries.

Yeah, right.

Who are we kidding?

Of course I wouldn't.

I know that reading another person's diary can reduce the amount of money you earn one day, add unwanted calories to your diet, and can result in tooth decay, intense blondness, and a whole bunch of other things nobody likes.

Trust me, I'm doing you a favor here. **Put down the diary and walk away slowly.**

Signed,

Jamie Kelly

P.S. Oh yeah, everything in here is true. I swear. At least, as true as it **needs** to be.

SUNDAY 01

Dear Dumb Diary,

So the carton says this stuff we buy is 2% milk. Am I the only one who wonders what the other 98% is? It could be **anything**, right? Mouthwash, udder sweat . . .

It just seems to me that what we **really** would like to know is what MOST of the stuff in there is — not just the 2% that's milk.

At our house, for my cereal I can use 2% milk, or coffee creamer, or skim milk, which my mom buys because she says it's helping her lose weight.

But she really **hates** drinking it, so my dad uses it in his coffee so she won't have to. He hates it, too, but he drinks it for her out of love.

Sometimes I feed it to the dogs out of my love for them both.

This is too much to think about first thing in the morning

At breakfast, I usually have one of these cereals to choose from:

We might have **WheatyOs**, which are like little dehydrated clown lips. Or we could have the **Fibergrunt Flakes**, which, based upon what I've heard about fiber, are eaten mostly because you also want to poo them. Or we might even have the **Frosted Crispy Wonderfuls**, which are purchased just for me — but my parents secretly eat them, so those are gone about four hours after they're purchased.

There's also always oatmeal, but I never eat that unless it's really cold out and I want to eat livestock feed. Or if the criminals that are holding me hostage are forcing me to eat it. (It's probably the **main way** you'll know that I'm being held hostage, and you should call the police.)

When cows dream, they dream of performing milk on Frosted Crispy Wonderfuls

And that's it. Those are my choices.

Well, on a **GOOD** day those are my choices. On a good day, Life lets me choose between the Fibergrunt Flakes and oatmeal. With skim milk.

I've always wished there was a way to demand that Life takes you out for **pancakes.**

While we're at it, I also DEMAND:

Cows that give stuff other than milk.

Cereal so big that you only need one single cereal.

This seems DOABLE

Comforters made out of pancake so you don't even have to get up.

I DON'T CARE if this is DOABLE OR NOT. SOMEBODY DO THIS

Dear Dumb Diary again,

I've decided not to do things like usual, Dumb Diary, because I want to tell you the entire story of **THE BIG WEIRD THING** without going day by day. So this is more like one gigantic diary entry that I'll just split up into chapters whenever I feel like it.

As the Very Beautiful Queen of this Diary, it is my right.

CHAPTER THREE

See? Just like that. At any given moment, I could just sur

CHAPTER FOUR

prise you with a new chapter.

CHAPTER SEVEN

I could even skip them. I might not even give them numbers. I might just give them names.

CHAPTER SYLVIA

Okay, names don't really work. Numbers. I'm going to use numbers.

CHAPTER EIGHT
EATING. ALL THE TIME, EATING.
WHAT IS IT WITH YOU?

The Big Weird Thing has a lot to do with food, so when you read this, it might seem like I spent a month or two doing nothing but eating. I did other interesting things, too, like sitting around and sleeping and stuff, but I just want to tell you about this one **BIG WEIRD THING**, so you'll have to imagine the other stuff.

CHAPTER NINE
NATURE'S BEAUTIFUL CRUELTY

Isabella says there's a **beautiful and elegant harmony** in Nature that makes it so your parents get old and feeble and unable to fight back at about the same time you want to throw them out of the house so you can keep it for **yourself**.

Unfortunately, she says, Modern Science has interfered with this gentle balance by giving us medicine and nutrition that keep our parents artificially **strong**. They're wrongly able to defend themselves for decades past what is really right.

We're all angry about this, sure, but it's hard for us to blame **Modern Science** for anything. It's given us the method by which we can miraculously turn a bowlful of various types of sands and powders into something as **magical** as cake. All we have to do is add heat and a raw egg, which is really pretty much just a liquefied chicken, and not something that you would usually add to dessert without Science telling you to.

Modern Science has also given us phones, computers, decorative pillows, and those X-ray machines at the airports that let us know if anybody is trying to get on an aircraft without **underwear** on.

We love **Modern Science**.

Seriously, would you want to live in a world without decorative pillows? Or blenders? Or have underwearless people sitting **right next to you** on a plane?

You know what we'd call smoothies if we didn't have blenders?

Fruit.

And who needs that?

When you think about it, many of our best modern foods are smoothies. Look at that bowl of soup: carrots, potatoes, onions, celery, beef, tomatoes. Soup is essentially a smoothie somebody made out of a **whole farm.** Yum.

OTHER SMOOTHIE FAVORITES

SNOWMAN SMOOTHIE

SKY SMOOTHIE

HAWAII SMOOTHIE

PRETTY LADY SMOOTHIE (VAMPIRES ONLY, PLZ)

I'm getting off track here. The whole discussion with Isabella about the elegance of throwing your parents **out in the cold** came up because of math class. I can explain.

Years ago, Isabella had a goldfish. She named it Golda. Back then, her mom wouldn't let her have a dog because they already had to take care of Isabella and Isabella's mean older brothers, and I've always had the impression that if there had been a way for Isabella's mom to leave one of those three people at the pet store, she would, but since she **couldn't**, she decided that she would leave all the dogs at the pet store instead.

Still, Isabella always felt that she could change her mom's mind. She thought that if she kept the fishbowl clean and the fish stayed healthy, then she would be able to talk her mom into getting a dog.

Oh — and she also felt that if she could just teach Golda a **trick**, then her mom would have to say yes.

One trick.

Adorable
Lil'
Intimidatin'
Isabella
♥

Goldfish are pretty. They're like tiny mermaids but with deformed faces. And they're relaxing to watch, but there's a reason you never see them guarding buildings, or herding sheep, or leading blind swimmers around in a lake.

They're **not smart** — not as smart as dogs anyway.

But that didn't stop Isabella.

She wanted to train Golda to **leap** out of the water like a dolphin. She would sit patiently and watch Golda, and every time Golda made a tiny move toward the surface, Isabella would hold a little flake of food just above the water and say, **"Jump!"**

And every time Golda didn't jump, Isabella would pull her out of the bowl and yell at her for it.

FISH FOOD

She had to secretly replace Golda **five times** before she rethought her methods. She had learned that yelling is pretty hard on a goldfish, even though she thought the first three fish were just pretending to be **asleep** to get out of jumping practice.

She also learned that rewards didn't really work any better than punishments because:

A) Goldfish can't hear underwater — screaming doesn't seem to help because they may not have ears.

B) Goldfish may not have dolphin jumping skills, even though they are both fish. (Yes, I know — dolphins are really mammals. **Not the time** to argue with her.)

C) The more recent goldfish may have had deep feelings for the earlier goldfish and now they would just never cooperate with Isabella out of revenge.

Isabella still had a very difficult time accepting these things, though, and continued to try to teach a goldfish a trick.

Just like my math teacher, Mr. Henzy.

GOLDA — OVER-SCOLDED

GOLDA 4 — OVER-SCOLDED

GOLDA 2 — OVER-SCOLDED

GOLDA THE 5TH — PROBABLY OVER SCOLDED

GOLDA THE THIRD — OVER-SCOLDED

GOLDA 6 — OVER-SCOLDED

I give Mr. Henzy a **lot** of credit for trying to teach me math.

I mean, **he** knows it's not going to happen, I know it's not going to happen, EVERYBODY knows it's not going to happen — but he still politely looks directly at me during the class, as if something might actually be sinking in for once. His faith in me is kind of **adorable** and **tragic** at the same time. One can't help but think of tiny Isabella dangling a sad little flake of fish food for her half-witted goldfish.

Is there a word for that? Maybe it's *"AWWWW-ful."*

Yes. Exactly. So Mr. Henzy did this **AWWWW-ful** thing where he tried to teach us **Personal Finance**, which is like the math you really and truly will **HAVE** to use to buy things and save money — not the kind of math where you might be walking down the street one day and suddenly have to know things about the area of a trapezoid.

To start things off, he had us write down our guesses of how much a house, a car, and a month's worth of groceries cost. Then he had us take those papers home and get our parents to sign them.

I know this seems crazy. These are things really only an adult needs to know about, and I won't be one of those for **centuries**.

Okay, maybe one century. **ABOUT** one century.

I love my parents, and I want them to have a good time, so why wouldn't I enjoy hearing the **trickling music** of their gentle laughter?

Well, maybe because, when they read my cost guesses, they **laughed so hard** that my mom had to go change and my dad couldn't breathe, which disturbed the dogs and made them **bite** each other.

I called Isabella to ask what her parents did when she showed them her paper, and she said they **grounded** her. Not for what she'd written down, but because she doesn't like being laughed at, and she decided that the best way to make them stop doing it involved her dad's bare foot and the **stomping** of it.

I would have called Angeline, but she probably guessed the answers perfectly exactly to the penny, and I really didn't want to hear how well she did.

It's one of the things I've learned about Angeline. Sure, on the outside, she's all beautiful and smart and kind to people, but when you go way down deep inside — way down deep — you discover that she's actually **more** beautiful and smart and kind.

This makes you hate her even more, but you then realize that even though that is the most natural reaction, it's terrible to hate somebody for being wonderful. And your hatred of Angeline for this will only make her look even better compared to you. So just by standing next to you, as you are becoming more terrible, she is actually improving — and you're **causing** it.

And that's not all. While you're standing there, simmering in your own hate gravy, **you are actually becoming worse** because that's what hate simmering does to a person.

So anyway, the safest assumption is that Angeline got the numbers right, and it's best to just live with that and not whip up a **whole batch of gravy** by asking about it.

CHAPTER TEN
FOR ONCE I WAS WRONG

Everything costs **WAY** more than I guessed and way more than Isabella guessed, too.

It appears as though I didn't fully understand money. I knew only one thing for sure: There's not enough to go around.

When they first invented money, I'm pretty sure old-timey people were all **excited** about it.

"Hey, we invented money! People are really going to **love** this," one of them correctly predicted.

"Yeah. Let's not make enough of it," said the other one with a mean laugh, and that's pretty much how they left things.

They know that we all want it, and yet for some messed-up reason, they won't make **enough** of it.

That's not how the guys making **turkeys** see things. I can't tell you exactly how many turkeys the world needs, but every time I'm at the grocery store, I see a **big freezer** of them wrapped up like frozen meteors. Without even doing the math, I'm quite confident that right this minute the world has at least **seven** more turkeys than we're ever going to need.

The guys making turkeys and the guys making the hundred-dollar bills need to **switch jobs** for a while.

The Raisin Guys, Weird Mustard Guys, and the Guys who make tools for my Dad can probably take a little time off, too.

That brings me back to my point: If we all had enough money, we could each afford our own house so that the temptation to **pitch our parents out the window** when they got old wouldn't be so overwhelming.

Don't get me wrong, Dumb Diary, I don't really want to overpower my parents and stuff them into that burlap bag in the garage and drag them 1.35 miles to that rest home on the corner of Maple Road and Adams Boulevard.

I've never even given it a **single thought**.

But right after a huge Thanksgiving meal would be a good time to get them. You know, when they're all **fat and groggy**. Right then.

I'm starting to understand why they made all those turkeys.

We've always known that we needed money, and over the years, Isabella and I have done many clever things to earn it.

We sold lemonade at a little lemonade stand.

We sold maps to where the **better** lemonade stands were.

We sold ~~used gross~~ vintage clothing door-to-door. (Sorry, Isabella's mom. She told me that you were going to throw it away anyway.)

We were also **professional musicians** singing on a street corner, even though some imbecile with no understanding of music sent an **ambulance** to see what was wrong with us.

But these small handfuls of pocket change don't add up to much money at all . . .

Not the kind of money Mr. Henzy was teaching us about.

For example, you know how everybody assumes that **horses** are more expensive than **cars** because they're prettier, and they can tell when you're sad, and they try to cheer you up by nuzzling you with their giant heads?

Yeah, well, it turns out that's not the case **AT ALL.**

Cars ridiculously cost a **TON OF MONEY,** and if you don't live in a place where you can walk everywhere, like some Lord of the Rings place, there's a pretty good chance you're going to need one.

It might be cheaper to just disguise a horse as a car...

Adults weirdly prefer the **ugly** cars.

I went to the car dealership with my dad once and noticed that adults can actually SEE THE COOL CARS from the desk where they're buying the ugly ones, but they go through with the ugly purchases anyway.

Why, adults? Why do you choose the ugliest version of everything all the time?

There's also fuel, maintenance, repairs, and insurance (which costs a bundle), and you need all of those as well, which is just silly.

What is **wrong** with adults?

GUESS WHICH ONE THE ADULT WILL CHOOSE

The Gorgeous and exciting CUPCAKE OR Her Homely and Quiet cousin, The Muffin

A TABLET FILLED WITH AWESOME GAMES AND MOVIES JUSTICE HORSE OR A TABLET THE DOCTOR TELLS THEM TO TAKE BECAUSE THEIR ORGANS ARE GROSS OR WHATEVER

WONDERFUL and TASTY LOLLYPOP OR FLY-SWATTER

OKAY THIS MIGHT NOT BE A FAIR COMPARISON

Mr. Henzy taught us that insurance is basically this deal where you bet a company that you **will** get in an accident, and they bet that you **won't**.

They charge you every single month whether you get into an accident or not, but if you get in one, they pay for the damages. Now this makes it sound like they're pretty cool with you and your **crashiness**, but after each accident, they start charging you more and more each month for the insurance. It's like they're starting to think that maybe you're getting into accidents on purpose, **just for the attention**.

If you need a loan from a bank to buy the car, they charge you interest on the loan, and by the time you pay them back, the car could actually cost you almost **twice** what the actual price was in the first place.

Here's how it works: Imagine if you gave somebody a piece of gum, and they had to give you back two (**new, unchewed**) pieces the next day. You'd get an extra piece of gum for **nothing**. That's how these loans work.

SCIENTIFIC DRAWING TO EXPLAIN IT

And if you **didn't** pay back the extra gum on time, they'd make sure that you could never borrow gum from anybody ever again. Also, they might come and take your **tongue**. (Truthfully, I'm really not sure how it would work with gum. This probably only works with money.)

Ew and if you ever DID get your tongue back, when you plugged it back in it would taste like everything it had touched at the bank.

And that's just for a **car**.

You're going to want someplace to live, too, and your antique, vitamin-gobbling parents are selfishly clinging to their house **forever**.

Those things cost more than I ever imagined, and you STILL need to pay for heat, Internet, water, Internet, electricity, Internet, and all that other junk.

And the stuff you buy eventually **breaks**. Unless you have somebody like my dad, who can **fix** your broken things — and then **fix them again** because he actually made them a little worse the first time he fixed them — you have to pay people to do this.

Plus, there's furniture and appliances and carpet and tons of stuff that you never even heard of.

And that's not counting the jillion little things. Like, you'll have to buy a brush to clean your toilet with. Toilets don't come with a brush, which I think shows how bad toilet makers are at thinking ahead. Seriously, toilet guys, did you think we were going to serve punch in these things?

STUFF YOU'LL NEED

(Every home must have these things)

JUNK DRAWER

This must include several items that nobody can identify.

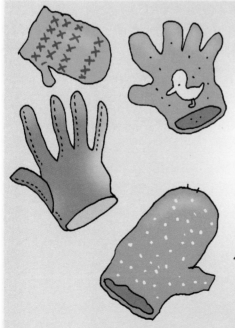

A MYSTERIOUS COLLECTION

of single gloves and mittens.

Where's the other one? Nobody knows.

They're probably at somebody else's house.

EVIDENCE OF AN OLD PET YOU NO LONGER HAVE.

Keep this for a while like you might replace it, then sell it at a garage sale.

HOLIDAY MIRTH

A SUPER UGLY OBJECT

that you got as a gift and only get out when the gift giver is coming over.

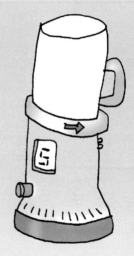

A THING THAT WOULD WORK IF YOU KNEW WHERE THE MISSING PART WAS

(It's in the junk drawer but you'll never realize it. Just throw it away)

CHAPTER ELEVEN
REALLY ITCHY, LIKE PORCUPINE UNDERPANTS

One night at dinner, as I picked at Mom's latest **Plateful of Disaster**, I asked my parents, "So, how much money do we have in the bank?"

It turns out that this is a pretty interesting question to ask your parents at dinner. It makes them act like their butts **itch**.

"Not enough," Dad said.

"Enough," Mom said at the exact same time, as if they had rehearsed this.

"Why are you asking, anyway?" Dad said suspiciously. "Did **Isadora** tell you to ask? Is she trying to get us to loan her money?"

"Who's Isadora?" I said.

"Your best friend. Big round glasses. Hairy arms. Criminal. **Isadora**."

"**ISABELLA**," I said.

"Oh, right. Isabella."

My dad does this all the time with names. I've heard him call our dog "Jamie":

"**Watch where you're walking,**" he once shouted helpfully to the guy delivering the pizza to our front door. "**Jamie pooped all over the front yard!**"

After I made him say Isabella's name out loud ten times, I explained that the reason I asked was for the Personal Finance thing we're doing in math. I told him that we were learning how much everything costs, and that it amazed me that we could afford **anything**.

Dad smiled widely. He clearly knew that this was one of those **"teachable moments"** parents are always looking for where you leave the door on your brain unlocked, so they can just stroll right in and leave something there.

"Here's the thing," he said with a warm, fatherly smile, "**we can't.** We can't afford anything."

Then he went back to eating.

I looked at Mom, and I must have appeared to be a bit **frightened**.

"There's more to it than that," she said. "We have a house and a car and food on the table. We have all the things we need, and a few extras, too. Your dad was just fooling around."

Dad made a grunty sound that we both recognized as the sound he makes when he disagrees but isn't willing to explain or argue. (We also recognize this sound as the one Stinker's intestines make if he eats soap, but this time it came from **Dad's face.**)

mom thought that I looked

a teeny bit frightened

I noticed that Mom looked concerned, but at the time, I believed it was due to her realization that she had married a man who occasionally sounded like **beagle bowels.**

There was more going on below the surface than I knew.

(Like with beagle bowels.)

CHAPTER TWELVE
ATTACK OF THE LIVING BLOND

Angeline, you might remember, **Cares About People**, which is one of the main ways she likes to annoy them.

She cares about how they're feeling, and how they're doing, and how things are going.

I SWEAR THIS IS TRUE: One time, Angeline asked somebody how they were, and she *actually listened to their response.*

It's not that being cared about is bad. It's just that those Really Caring People make you feel bad about yourself because you're not as caring.

Being less caring like this makes you less annoying to others.

Being less annoying to others makes more of them care about you. This, in turn, makes you feel even worse because now even **MORE** people are more caring than you are.

Sometimes I think you just can't win with nice people.

COMPLAIN
BRAG
GRIPE
BELLYACHE
GROAN

PEOPLE. When I say "HOW ARE YOU?" I EXPECT YOU TO JUST SAY "**FINE**" And move on...

Angeline always sits with us at lunch.

Angeline could sit anywhere in the cafeteria she wanted, and people would run and get her anything she asked for — their lunches, their firstborn children, high-priced gum in those cool packages. No sacrifices would be too much to make to the **Goddess of Popularity**.

But she sits with us.

Because she likes us, she says.

See how annoying?

Isabella and I don't even like us that much.

Isabella once had a theory that Angeline's popularity was like head lice and that we could catch it just by being close to her. She even made Angeline switch clothes with her at lunch one time and wear her beautiful blond hair tucked up under a dirty hat.

Isabella wore Angeline's clothes and a wig, but it didn't fool anybody. We decided that if we could bottle and sell whatever **Magical Popularity** Angeline has going for her, we'd make a fortune.

Privately, we agreed that we'd be willing to just bottle and sell Angeline.

At some point during lunch, we became aware of a high-pitched sound that seemed to be coming from the direction of Angeline's immaculately glossed lips. It turned out that she was, in fact, talking to us.

"One of the main health issues we're facing is obesity," she began, and we **groaned** and **slammed our heads** against the table because Angeline had lectured us about this before.

"Angeline, you're not fat," Isabella said, lifting her head from the table and adjusting her glasses, then adding, **"Yet."**

"What do you mean by that?" Angeline said. I could tell she was a little **miffed**, which is about as angry as Angeline gets.

"Angeline, you talk about obesity like it actually affects you," Isabella said. "**YOU** are not fat. So stop worrying about it. You won't be fat like your mom until you're her age. What is she, like, eighty-five?" Isabella asked, and it kind of sounded like she said that last word twice, probably due to the fact that Angeline's mouth had fallen open as large as the entrance of a cave, and it was causing a mild **echo**.

"My mom's not fat," Angeline said after the initial shock had worn off.

"Okay, okay," Isabella said. "Your mom's not fat."

Angeline nodded angrily.

Isabella added, "So who is that we see driving you to school? **Your pet elephant?**"

okay pretty mean, Isabella, but also pretty fun to draw so I'll allow it

Angeline's mouth fell open even further than before. With a flashlight, I might have been able to tell what she had for breakfast.

Isabella just smiled at Angeline.

"She's not fat, you know," Angeline said through gritted, pearly teeth.

"Of course she's not," Isabella said. "I was just kidding. It wouldn't matter if she was. Honestly, I can't think of anything that I'm less interested in than how much people weigh. In your mom's case, she just happens to be as **horribly perfect** as you are. But here's the thing: When thin people like you tell fat people that they're fat, it doesn't make them want to lose weight. It makes them want to eat you thin people. You're just **too perfect** to talk about this subject."

"I'm not talking about how people look," Angeline said. "I know that everybody looks different, and sometimes it doesn't matter much what they eat. People can look good at every size. I'm talking about how **healthy** they are." Angeline's sparkling eyes and velvety voice cut through me like sparkling, velvety chainsaws. She eyed the can of root beer in front of me.

"I have an idea I want to tell you about," she went on.

Heck
I'd
do it

I admit, I had gotten into the habit of bringing cans of soda pop in for lunch. (I recently learned that they call it **POP** some places, and **SODA** other places. I like using the full name because it shows how much I love it.)

I knew that soda pop wasn't the best thing for me. But it's just so bubbly and refreshing, it makes you think that the only reason that everything isn't carbonated is that Nature just never thought of it.

I also really enjoy burping. Burps are like secret messages in **stomach language** that my body is sending out to the world. "Hello," my stomach is probably saying, or "Hey, remember when you ate this?"

And after a lifetime of dealing with my mom's horrible cooking, I've become an expert on what flavors cancel out other horrible flavors. Root beer can cure a lot of them, including **Cafeteria Chicken Taco**, which is what they were serving that day at lunch. Winding up in a Cafeteria Chicken Taco is pretty much the worst thing that can ever happen to a chicken. Chickens tell one another **scary stories** about it around campfires.

This little soda pop habit of mine made me feel like the target of every nutritional message anywhere, but I didn't care. Coke, Pepsi, 7Up — I liked them all, and I was concerned that Angeline's obesity idea might impact my **delicious, burpy beverages**.

"And I think there may be some **money** in it," Angeline added quietly.

Isabella and I looked at each other and **blinked** several times as we tried to absorb this. Angeline was talking about doing something, not just for the good of the world, or the good of humanity, or the good of catnanity — that's like humanity, but for cats (it might not really be a thing). She was talking about doing something for the **cash**.

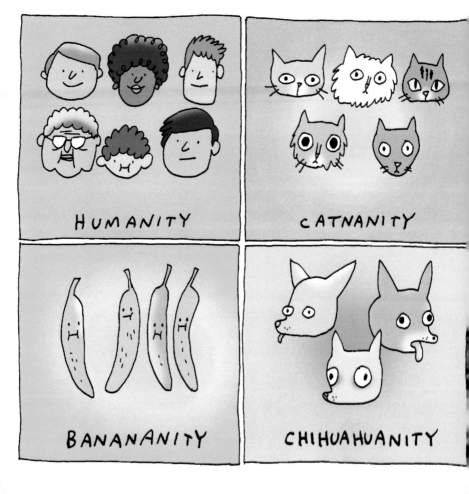

HUMANITY

CATNANITY

BANANANITY

CHIHUAHUANITY

"**I'm in,**" Isabella chirped immediately.

"Wait a second," I said. "You were just giving Angeline all kinds of grief about this. You can't just change your mind like that."

Light glinted across Isabella's glasses in such a way that I couldn't see her eyes. That's always disconcerting. It's like talking to a **Stormtrooper**.

"Jamie," she said, "money changes things for me, in the same way that a penguin can change a day at the beach for a killer whale. It's what I am. It's what I believe in. I'm not going to lie to you, Jamie. There is a price I would sell you for, and it's **not as high** as you think."

"Just tell me it's higher than what a car costs," I said.

"It's more than what many cars cost," she said, and patted my hand. I jerked it away.

"Money can't buy happiness," I wisely reminded her in my ultra-wise wisdom.

"We've all heard that saying a million times," she scoffed. "But we've never heard it from somebody who needed money. If you offer a dollar to a broke person, they **won't** turn it down. Do you think they'll ever say, *No, thanks. I'm afraid that buying myself something to eat with that dollar might not make me happy?* Grow up, Jamie."

She was right. In a horrible, horrible, horrible way, she was right. We don't need all the money in the world, but we need **some** of it.

And maybe Angeline really **did** have a good idea. I mean, it had to happen sooner or later, right?

CHAPTER THIRTEEN
THE IDEA

Angeline's bedroom is clean. It's pink and small — Angeline's parents are not rich — but everything is neat and organized, and there are a lot of tiny things neatly arranged.

"How do you keep things so *undestroyed*?" Isabella asked with genuine curiosity as she looked around at all the undestroyed items.

There was a tiny glass unicorn on Angeline's dresser.

"Look at those frail little glass legs," Isabella said with wonder. "I can feel them starting to break just by staring at them."

"Let's not stare at them, then," Angeline said, motioning for us to join her on the floor. "Let's look at this instead. This is the idea I wanted to tell you about."

She slid a box out from under her bed and opened it with great ceremony, beaming.

"What do you think?" she asked proudly.

It was a **paper plate** with writing on it.

We heard Isabella opening the front door before we realized she had stood up and **left the room.** She was halfway down the front steps before we caught up to her.

"You didn't even let me tell you about it," Angeline whined.

"You said this idea was worth money," Isabella said. "A paper plate with writing on it? I know a **bad idea** when I see one."

"We came all the way over here. We should at least let her do her little presentation," I said.

Isabella dragged her feet as hard as she could, groaning loudly as she plodded from the front porch all the way back to Angeline's room.

She flopped down on the floor as hard as if somebody had scooped out her insides and replaced them with barbecue charcoal.

"Let's hear it, Cupcake," she moaned.

She also reminded me of a deflated pool toy

"So," Angeline began, cheerfully unaware that the name **"Cupcake"** is an insult. (Although as I write this, I'm not sure why, since they're delicious and beautiful and everybody likes them . . .)

"So, you know how obesity is a problem," she began, "but people may not always know how to address it —"

"You address it like this: *TO FATTYPANTS*," Isabella cut in.

Angeline ignored the interruption and Isabella's accompanying snorts.

"So, with these specially printed plates, people are reminded of what they **should** be eating," she went on. "See, it's like a pie chart, except there's not much room for pie." She giggled, absurdly pleased with her own lame joke.

Angeline held up a plate and pointed to the different sections with a long, graceful finger (which looked like a swan finger, if swans had fingers). There was a diagram showing how much of each meal should be protein, how much should be vegetables, and so on.

when she picks her nose it probably looks like a ballet

AS IF SHE DOES

FRUIT GRAINS VEGETABLES PROTEIN

"How do we make **money** off this?" Isabella demanded.

Angeline smiled. "Well, we come up with the design — I know Jamie can do that, she's so talented — and we sell the idea to a company that manufactures plates. I know that you can do that part, Isabella. You're very persuasive. I mean — you guys can do so much."

She was manipulating us like dough. Like the sweet, delicious dough that we are. And she was baking us into the type of delicious cookies you can only get from dough like us. And she was putting sprinkles of us on top of us, and — forget it. **I'm hungry.** I want some cookies. I'll pick this up in the next chapter, called . . .

when you are so Hungry the entire world suddenly looks like a cookie

CHAPTER FOURTEEN
OKAY, I HAD COOKIES AND CAN WRITE AGAIN

Isabella and I discussed how much better Angeline's plate idea could be, if it wasn't drawn so badly by Angeline, and if it was pitched by somebody better at pitching than Angeline.

"**I'm right here, guys,**" Angeline said. "I can hear you."

I patted her hand softly. "Angeline, it's important that you realize that we know that."

"What would somebody pay for plates like this?" Isabella asked, getting to the point. That's how she likes her points: **gotten to.**

"Maybe only a little bit more than they're already paying for plates," Angeline said. "But if the manufacturers pay us a little for each one, it could add up."

Angeline watched Isabella stand up and move slowly toward the door.

The backward walk of the displeased

"**AND** Mr. Henzy will give us extra credit for this," she added, batting her eyelashes out of habit before remembering that her eyelash batting doesn't work on us. "He'd love to see us do a project that would increase our real-life personal finances."

"Do you think it could bring my grade up to a D?" Isabella asked hopefully.

"It might. What's your grade now?"

"It's a pretty bad grade," Isabella said. "It's like if you concentrated your hardest on intentionally forgetting everything you were ever taught."

"Like an F?" Angeline asked. "Like you're failing?"

"It's a **little lower** than that," Isabella said.

WORDS

MATHS

DATES

ISABELLA'S BRAIN -O- MATIC

CAFETERIA-QUALITY COLE SLAW OUT

SCHOOL STUFF IN

"I didn't know there was anything lower than failing," Angeline said, blinking her wide, innocent eyes.

Isabella chuckled.

"There's an entire **WORLD** of grades below what you surface dwellers know," Isabella said. "While you're floating around up here in the clouds, among the A's and B's, you have no idea what's going on down in the G's and H's."

"Isabella got a J once in math. Basically, that means that she couldn't count to one," I explained.

"I totally could," Isabella said. "I just didn't **want** to."

"So, what do you say, Angeline?" I asked. "Will this get her up to a D?"

"It might," she said with a shrug.

QUEEN OF THIS DARK REALM

"I like this," Isabella said, waggling the plate at Angeline. "It's a little bit like **stealing**, but also a little bit like **cheating**."

Of course it was nothing like either of those things, but when Isabella is in a good mood, sometimes it's best to just let it go without an argument.

And so, without any more preparation, we plunged into **The Big Weird Thing**.

Once, when we were little, I told Isabella if you take the bulb out, the electricity would leak out all over the floor.

It made her so happy that I never told her I was kidding.

CHAPTER FIFTEEN
THE PRICE WE HAVE TO PAY

I never really know what to expect when I drag my tail into math class. It might be **boring**, but on the other hand, it could be **terrible**.

This time it was terrible. Again.

Mr. Henzy made us guess at the cost of a college education. Again, we had to take our papers home and get our parents to sign them.

Isabella said she wasn't going to fall for it this time, so her plan was to just ask her parents what it would cost, write down a number a little higher than that, and have them sign it. She had not yet decided if she would be **stomping** on her dad's foot anyway.

That sounded like a good idea to me — not the stomping part, just the asking part — so I gave it a shot at dinner.

"What's it going to cost you two to put me through college?" I asked just as my dad was trying to squeeze down a bite of one of my mom's casserole-shaped objects. "And let's make it someplace good, like a really good college. Something deluxe. One where they grow ivy on the buildings."

A lot of people credit Dr. Heimlich with the brilliance of his maneuver — you know, the one where your mom gets behind your dad and squashes his guts with one big sudden **squeeze**. And the good doctor deserves a lot of credit. Think how many lives that move has saved.

What they never give him enough credit for is the hilarious **popping sound** a clump of casserole makes when it's forced out your dad's trachea at eighty miles an hour.

It should be called **Heimlich's Hysterical Champagne Bottle of Comedy.**

PORP!

After Dad recovered from being maneuvered, he made it clear why he had choked.

"Jamie, parents can't always afford college for their kids. Sometimes kids have to get loans to afford college," he said, and his voice had a sad, serious tone to it.

"And scholarships," Mom added. "Students often try to get scholarship money from the college, based on good grades or special abilities."

"So . . . **how much** is it going to cost?" I asked again.

Dad stared down at his casserole, and it probably stared back. It's always possible that Mom baked something's eye into dinner.

"Jamie, we're going to make it work for you," he said, and he stood up and walked away from the table.

I looked at Mom, and she faked a smile. I have no idea why people try that. There's nothing more **obvious** than a faked smile.

In the corner of the room, Stinker ate the thing Dad had coughed up.

Then I watched him eat it a couple more times, and it struck me that he was doing a pretty good job of **dramatizing** just how I felt.

AMAZING SCIENCE

Things just don't get any grosser the more times they're coughed up!

coughed up one time

coughed up six times

coughed up fifty times

coughed up 112 times

coughed up 467 times

coughed up one million times

I went up to my room and worked on Angeline's plates. There's something about the smell of **pencil shavings** and **glitter** that always makes me feel better. I came up with a few ideas:

I showed them to Angeline and Isabella the next day at lunch.

"Is this all you've got?" Isabella asked, which is the perfect question to ask somebody if your goal is to destroy their self-confidence. This never works on me, however, because Isabella destroyed whatever I had left of that years ago, and in its place I grew a hard, turtle-ish shell.

"I think they're great," Angeline said, her eyes **shimmering annoyingly** with excitement.

"So how do we test them?" I asked.

Isabella grabbed Dicky Flartsnutt by the collar and pulled him over to our table. Dicky, you might recall, Dumb Diary, is our very good friend who we love and who is a dork.

Isabella had him look at the plates, which he did with the enthusiasm that only dorks have for things like paper plates and that rainbow you sometimes get with a garden hose.

"They're plates," he said, getting right to the heart of it.

Other things he really really really really loves

unwrapping cheese slices

sharpening pencils down to nubs

just standing there not being teased

"If you had to eat off these, would it make you want to be less fat?" Isabella asked.

Angeline interrupted.

"No. No. Hang on. That's not the right question. Dicky, first tell us, do you like **the look** of these plates?" she asked gently.

"Yes. Jamie drew on them. I can tell."

"That's right. But what if Jamie hadn't drawn on them?"

"Then I guess they'd be blank."

I interrupted.

"Dicky, we want to sell plates like these to people like your mom. Do you think she'd buy these? You know, to set up balanced meals for you?"

"Yes," he said, and Isabella released him with a little shove.

Isabella Loves Dicky but doesn't realize he's not very SHOVE-RESISTANT

"They're a hit!" Angeline squealed, making tiny rapid claps directly in front of her face.

"A **HIT**?" Isabella scoffed. "Because Dicky likes them? Dicky likes the sound of the Velcro on his shoes, too."

"They're not a hit exactly, Angeline," I said. "Not yet. We have some work to do."

In the weeks that followed, we tried to figure out how to really make the plates a genuine hit. Angeline started researching companies that made paper plates, and I worked on improving the designs.

Isabella watched a lot of Netflix movies about companies or jobs or something — she never really explained exactly how that was helping, but I'm sure she was learning **important stuff**.

I must have redrawn the designs for the plates a **million** times, after learning what proportions of protein, grains, vegetables, and other stuff the experts recommended.

There was only one thing left to do. We had to actually make some plates and **test them out**.

LATE - NIGHT STUDYING

First, we needed a way to get the images on the plates. It turned out that running them through the copier at school was just about the simplest, easiest way to **jam it forever** and make it **catch on fire**.

We explained to Assistant Principal Devon (my Uncle Dan) what we were doing with the plates as he was vacuuming up the copier toner that the firemen had spilled all over the floor.

He said that maybe Miss Anderson (my art teacher) could make it an art project and have all the kids decorate their plates themselves with nonpoisonous markers and try them out at lunch. (Assistant principals are always really interested in **not poisoning kids.**)

Using my designs, each kid would draw the proportions on their plate, and then the cafeteria workers would put the food on the plates based on the design.

some will do a better job than others

And that's what happened.

I make it sound like this all happened fast, but it actually took a while to get everything together.

Miss Anderson didn't really want to interrupt her class schedule with the plates because she had **very big**, **very important** plans for her students to create some spectacular masterpieces featuring macaroni glued to something. You know, just like the great works of art you see in museums.

DUCK

SNAKE

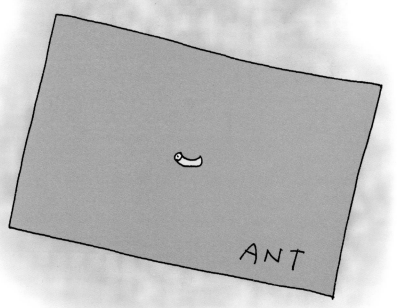

ANT

But Uncle Dan talked her into it, possibly because I think she has an adult crush on him, which is illegal because he's married to my Aunt Carol, but I'm not going to say anything because we **ARE** getting our plates after all.

Sorry, Aunt Carol, you're on your own with this one. Hope there's not a big awful divorce coming up.

Hey, since I was invited to their wedding, am I **automatically** invited to their divorce?

Probably.

The Baker probably makes it TASTE KIND OF BITTER

The day finally arrived, and we proudly watched as kids lined up in the cafeteria with their HEALTH-O-PLATES.

Yes. That's what Angeline calls them. I know, I know.

Angeline took careful notes. Isabella snapped pictures with her phone.

We proudly watched as the lunch staff precisely glopped the foods on the plates in the correct proportions.

I **proudly** nodded at Uncle Dan as he **proudly** winked at me. This was a great idea, and he **proudly** knew it.

We **proudly** watched as kids walked to find their seats, stopping only briefly to slide the glop they didn't like directly into the trash cans before they sat down.

"No, no, no," Angeline said as she stopped Mike Pinsetti in mid-glop sliding. "The idea is that you eat it **all**. You eat everything on your plate. See, the plates help you balance your meal."

"**Why?**" Mike asked blankly.

"For your health," Angeline said, with her arms spread wide as if she was going to hug everybody's health all at once.

"I don't really like my health," Mike said. He tried to walk around her, but she moved back in front of him.

Pinsetti is kind of a bully and weighs two hundred pounds more than Angeline, but for some reason, he stopped dead and listened to her.

"You don't like your health?" she asked.

"Well, I kinda like it." He shrugged. "But if my health is going to be a huge jerk all the time about what I eat, then, like, **forget him**."

We scanned the cafeteria. Nobody was eating everything on their plates. Nobody was even paying attention to their plates.

Except Dicky.

Dicky ate everything, and he ate it all alphabetically, just in case alphabetical eating was a thing. I'm guessing he thought it might be because vitamins are alphabetical.

Isabella snapped a couple photos of the rejected food in the trash cans.

"These plates don't work," Isabella said. "Nobody will obey a plate."

I looked down in the trash. Angeline dragged herself over and dropped her little notepad in.

"They even threw away the salads," I said. "I mean, some of the other stuff is gross, but who doesn't like a salad?"

"I don't," Isabella said. "Salads aren't food. Salads are what food **eats**."

ISABELLA'S FOOD CHAIN

"That's dumb," Angeline mumbled. **"You're dumb."**

The HEALTH-O-PLATE failure had hit Angeline harder than we knew. Angeline never called people dumb. Not even dumb people. One time, we went on a field trip to a farm and saw a horse that could only gallop backward, and Angeline wouldn't even call **him** dumb. She called him "differently stabled."

She was really depressed.

"A salad is just a pile of leaves," Isabella said. "When my dad is out working in the yard, he throws away bags and bags of salad. Stop by and eat one anytime you like, Angeline."

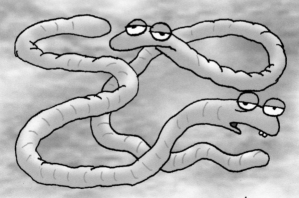

Angeline won't even call worms DUMB.

She says they're great at solving problems like making sure birds get to eat and kids have something to throw at their sisters.

"So dumb," Angeline repeated, staring at the floor. It was hard to tell who her criticism was aimed at.

"But you can put salad dressing on them," I said to Isabella, still trying to make a case for salads. "That's just goop, and you **love** goop."

"There aren't even that many good ones to choose from," Isabella said. "A few different kinds of ranch, some vinaigrettes, Thousand Island. We have a million different ways to make a sandwich but only a few kinds of tolerable salad dressings, and none of them are tasty enough to make me eat what's basically a floral arrangement."

Decoration

Food

Angeline shuffled off, muttering to herself. There's really nothing quite as sad as a **perky blond** in the dumps. It's like seeing a bunny dipped in tar, or a Christmas cookie on the floor of a public bathroom.

I probably should have offered her a sip of my 7Up, but that would have meant that I would have had one sip less, and that **wasn't going to work** for me.

What's sadder than a Sad Angeline?

Giraffe with a neck condition

Skinny Santa

Dirty Clown chewing on your toothbrush

Yeah this is more horrifying than Sad

Later, in Mr. Henzy's class, he asked how our **HEALTH-O-PLATES** experiment had gone. We had to confess that it was a huge failure. We told him that nobody was really very interested in our creation.

He was actually pretty sweet about it all.

"Things like that usually fail," he said.

"Hey, thanks for the warning!" Isabella shouted. "By the way, when you warn people, that means **YOU TELL THEM IN ADVANCE.**"

CAUTION THAT TOP STAIR WAS SLIPPERY

Right you are, Isabella

"Don't get me wrong," he said. "I just mean that many ideas don't work at first. Things sometimes need to be modified or retested. Diamonds don't look that great when you dig them up. They have to be **polished** — then they're spectacular."

"Cat turds don't look great when you dig them up, either," Isabella said. "But they don't change much when you try to polish them."

"Do we still get **extra credit**?" I asked, trying to find something positive in this whole mess.

"Yes, of course," he said. "You actually learned more by failing than succeeding."

"Thanks," Isabella said. "Nice job encouraging us to **fail**."

I looked over at Angeline, who had said nothing during the entire exchange. She didn't smile. She didn't blink. She wasn't even trying that hard to smell good, which is one of her main things.

MILD LETTUCE SMELL

NOT EVEN THAT GREAT REALLY

CHAPTER SIXTEEN
THIS IS WHERE I FOUND OUT WHAT THE DEAL WAS

That night, Aunt Carol came over for dinner. Uncle Dan had to leave town for some assistant principal convention, where they teach them to be better assistant principals.

I began to tell her about the HEALTH-O-PLATE tragedy, but she already knew about it. Even though it was a colossal embarrassment, she thought it was great that the three of us were already thinking about earning money for college.

"You're really going to need it," she said. "Especially Angeline. You know that her dad got fi —"

Mom **kicked** Aunt Carol so hard one of her earrings fell off.

I lunged for it, of course, because Stinker believes that anything that falls on the floor is food. I've seen a few fashion items that have been **run through** a beagle. It really doesn't improve most of them.

But Stinker didn't snap at it, so I was able to return it to Aunt Carol uneaten.

"What were you saying about Angeline?" I asked.

"Nothing," Mom said, but it wasn't the **"nothing"** where there isn't anything there. It was the **"NOTHING"** where there's so much of something there that you can't stand it. It was the kind of nothing that is the **exact opposite** of nothing.

"I think I should know, Mom," I said. "I'm old enough to handle big things."

"Okay," she said with a sigh. "Angeline's dad got **fired**, and things are really tight for them right now. We're a little better off, but as of this moment, we don't have enough money to pay for you to go to college. When Grandma died, we thought there might be a little something for you to inherit, but after her expenses, there was hardly anything left. She said that she wanted you to have a **bracelet** of hers that might have been worth something, but **we can't find it**. We think it must have gotten lost when we packed up her things."

I swallowed hard.

Guess I was wrong.

I really **wasn't** old enough to handle big things. Not all at once, shoved in my face like that. And up my nose and under my eyelids and down my throat and in my ears.

"That's why Angeline cared so much about her plate idea. She really needs to make money," I said quietly.

"Don't share this information with anybody, Jamie," Mom said sternly. "I'm trusting you not to talk to anybody about it. Not Angeline, and especially not Isabella."

"Okay," I said. "What about Isabella? Can I tell her?"

"Not **ANYBODY**."

"Okay. I understand. I promise," I said.

The Information Highway

But here's the thing about promises:

If you promise somebody something and they **don't** believe that you'll keep the promise, then when you break that promise, it's not that big of a deal: They weren't counting on you anyway, so nobody gets blamed for anything.

If you promise somebody something and they DO believe you, but they **SHOULDN'T** have believed you, then when the promise is broken they really should have known better. It's not **your** fault that they didn't.

If you promise somebody something and they believe you, and they had every reason to believe you, and you really intended to keep the promise, then the only reason the promise could have been broken was because of something that was totally out of your control. And who could blame you for something out of your control?

I'm not saying I broke that promise to my mom, I'm just saying it's important to understand how promises actually work, and I'm **never to blame**.

The next morning at school, I saw Angeline filling her water bottle at the drinking fountain. She does this every day, many times a day, because she is responsible about not wasting plastic bottles, and like so many people these days, she needs **constant hydration**.

You never see people in old photos or movies carrying water bottles around, but nowadays everybody does, even though I think people a long time ago used to work harder and would have been thirstier.

My friends often take a water bottle with them in the car, going between their house and someplace where there is water, as if maybe something will happen in the car that will cause them to have **life-threatening thirst**.

There are fish who drink less water.

Anyway, Angeline was filling her bottle again, but she wasn't holding it at the right angle where the water would enter the bottle flawlessly, like she usually does. She wasn't even smiling at the water, and Angeline smiles at **everything**.

She was getting some water in the bottle, some on her hand, some on the floor. And she was looking nowhere, staring at nothing. Her eyes even seemed less blue, less twinkly. I think she may have been shedding some of her eyelashes, which would be very bad news for the janitors, since they would have to rake them up.

"**Good news,**" I blurted out involuntarily.

UNANGELINISH POSTURE

HAIR AS BAD AS MINE

NO SHIMMERY GLIMMER ON LIPS

JANGLY THINGS NOT JANGLING

SOMEHOW SHE IS MAKING ALL THE THINGS AROUND HER LOOK BROWNER

I could taste the **lie** forming in my mouth. I could feel it kicking around. I was sweating. It hurt.

I didn't want to do it. But she was so sad. She was so worried. With one immense labor pain, I gave birth to a lie baby.

"My dad spoke to somebody he knows who makes paper plates, and they're interested in our **HEALTH-O-PLATES.**"

It seemed as though time slowed down for a moment, and I could see the lie swirling around in the air between us. Angeline was staring at it. The color returned to her eyes, her cheeks reddened, and she activated the enzyme in her body that makes her smell like strawberries.

← RADISH AND CORN FRAGRANCE

CREAKING SOUND OF EYELASHES ERUPTING

THIS MAY ACTUALLY BE HOW RAINBOWS ARE CREATED

And then: **the sound.**

It was like a squeal that steadily rose in pitch and volume into something like a scream, but more musical than that — like if a flute screamed. And then it got louder, and the sound of laughter seemed to be added to the scream, and every container of spoiled milk in a two-mile radius suddenly became fresh again.

She hugged me and waggled me around like a doll until the bell rang and she had to skip merrily to class.

I knew it was a lie, but for the moment, it seemed like the **right thing to do.**

I turned to go to class and walked straight into Isabella.

Angeline's squeals of delight have been known to cause fairies to be spontaneously born in the clouds above the school

"What was that about?" she asked.

"You heard that?" I said, and I realized that I was about to lie to my best friend, which I should never do. Isabella almost **invented** lying to best friends, and she can tell when anyone is doing it.

"We all heard it, Jamie. And look at you. You've been **freshly waggled.**"

It's pretty easy to tell when somebody has just received a waggling.

"I told her that my dad knows somebody in the paper plate business, and they might be interested in our HEALTH-O-PLATES."

"What's his name?"

"It's not a him. It's a her. Her name is Kirsten Hall."

The Unwaggled

The Waggled

The Permanently Waggled

Just like that, I had used one of Isabella's own techniques against her. Years ago, Isabella taught me to have a couple **FASTFAKENAMES** ready, just in case someone asks. The names have to be believable, and you have to practice saying them. Stalling for a name will always give you away.

My female **FASTFAKENAME** is Kirsten Hall.

I have an entire assortment. My male **FASTFAKENAME** is Bob Peterson. My fake **FASTFAKENAME** for myself is Jenny Ryan. My **FASTFAKENAME** for a pet is Twinkle. I can go on and on.

"So we might get **paid**?" Isabella asked, her fingers clenching imaginary money. (She doesn't even realize she does that.)

"We might," I said, looking her in the eye. Not for too long, of course, because that makes it obvious you're lying. It's almost as bad as avoiding eye contact completely. There's an exact amount of time that's right. Like half a second.

"Cool," Isabella said, and we started walking to class.

Lying is good, I said to myself, carefully making sure not to say it out loud, since I've learned that's another excellent way to get caught.

ALSO LOOKING LIKE
THIS WILL GET YOU CAUGHT

CHAPTER SEVENTEEN
YOU'RE GOING TO NEED BIGGER REINDEER

Every single day after that, Angeline had a new idea for the plates.

Every day.

Every. Single. Day.

"Let's make one for kids who can't read yet."

"Let's make one for kids with food sensitivities."

"Let's make one for kids with different religious requirements."

And Isabella would nod in agreement, and I would have to go home and make the stupid things.

"Any word from your dad's friend yet?" Angeline would ask. "Should we have a meeting with her or something?"

The whole thing reminded me of **the Easter Bunny.**

When I was little, my parents told me about a happy little bunny that came every Easter and hid baskets full of chocolate and jelly beans for all the children.

Pretty good story, except that the neighbor lady had a pet bunny.

His name was Bouncyboy and he was too stupid to even react to his own name, much less have his act together enough to prepare baskets of candy. It's true, at first he **seemed** to be pretty generous with the black jelly beans, but those weren't really jelly beans.

So, deep down, I knew the whole story was a lie. But every Easter, there would be a basket of candy for me, so I didn't ask a lot of questions.

"The Easter Bunny is coming," Mom would say in the weeks before Easter, and she'd be all excited and playful.

"Oh. Right. Sure thing, Mom," I would say, and we kept up that **Gigantic Yearly Lie** until we all just ran out of the energy to maintain it.

So I figured that's how it would go with the HEALTH-O-PLATES. I'd lie for a little longer, Angeline would eventually run out of energy, and the entire issue would just fade away, like the Easter Bunny.

But it didn't fade away.

It got worse.

And it served as a great example of why people should never talk to people.

One day, I walked into the school and found myself strolling down the hallway that passes in front of the school office. I realized, once it was **too late** to turn around, that Angeline, Aunt Carol, and Uncle Dan were standing there talking, which, you'll remember I pointed out earlier, is a bad thing for people to do.

I knew they were going to ask me about the plates. There was no way they weren't.

There was only one logical thing to do.

I turned around and quickly smashed my math book up into my face. Nobody would question me if I had a **bloody nose**. I'd have to go take care of it — right?

Turns out that noses don't always bleed that easily. So now my whole face hurt, my nose wasn't bleeding, and I still had to walk past them.

Angeline waved like crazy and pranced like a pretty little goat.

"Hi, everybody," I said, and kept walking. I tried to look like one of those celebrities who had committed a **recent crime** and was trying to get past the reporters to her limousine.

"Running late," I added, rubbing my nose, which hurt for the rest of the day.

How to look just like a celebrity in photographs

I only got away briefly. Later on, at lunch, Angeline was waiting to **pounce**.

"Did your dad talk to his friend yet?" she asked.

"Angeline," I began, surprised at how nasal my voice sounded from the book slamming, "we might not be able to totally depend on this, you know."

"I don't want to get into it," she said. "But I kind of **have** to depend on this. And when it becomes a huge success, it's going to be that much better because we did it together. Best friends, **together**."

Isabella's expression was unchanged, but I'm sure I heard a tiny, cruel laugh escape her lips. It was so small and so quiet that maybe I was the only one who could hear it. It was the kind of laugh that only a friend can hear: *silent but friendly*.

"**Together**," I repeated, and I tried my hardest to use my mind to make my nose bleed so I could leave the table. Then I tried making Angeline's nose bleed.

I noticed that Dicky's nose bled a little, and I wondered if my mind had accidentally gone up his nose, but I then I remembered that his nose always bleeds when he drinks milk, which he's not supposed to do and which he does daily.

My nose is just way too **tough**.

By the time I got home, I realized that something had to change. While we were eating dinner, I turned to my dad for help.

"Dad, somebody called for you. Her name was Kirsten Hall. She said it was something about plates," I said.

"Plates? Where was she from?"

Mom got excited.

"I can't believe you **remembered** that I wanted new plates for our anniversary!" she said, throwing her arms around him. "You're the best."

This was not what I had planned. I just wanted to put the **fake name** in Dad's head and tell him that it had something to do with him and plates. That way, later I could get him to nod or something when I was explaining to Angeline that the deal wasn't going through.

"Oh, right, plates," he would say, distracted by the TV. "Yeah. Something something plates."

This would be enough to convince Angeline that I had been telling the truth — she's too polite to question him for details.

But I **wasn't prepared** for Mom's reaction. She assumed Dad was buying new table settings.

And if I was underprepared for Mom's reaction, Dad's was even harder to anticipate.

Without hesitation, he turned to me and said, "Well, Jamie. You've kind of ruined the surprise, but yes, I was talking to that woman about getting Mom new plates for our anniversary."

Be warned

GENTLE TENDER CARESSES

some Moms develop weird love of plates and stuff like that

I was shocked, disgusted, and a little **impressed**. Dad had pulled off a huge lie with practically **no effort**.

"Did you get her number?" he asked.

"She said you had it," I said.

"Oh, right. Of course," Dad said, even smoother.

"What's her accent?" I asked, just to check the level of **smoothness** here.

"German," he responded easily.

He was so smooth I could have **ice-skated** down his back.

I nodded at him slowly and took a bite of my salad. I wondered how deep we were going into this lie. Just then, Stinker lay in the corner and farted, which was perhaps the only **sincere and genuine** thing expelled into the room that evening.

The only time you know for sure that somebody is sharing the truth is when they fart

FFFFT

maybe this should be on a wise decorative wall hanging?

No

CHAPTER EIGHTEEN
THE WORST THING SHE'S EVER DONE

They say the secret of martial arts is anticipating what your opponent will do before they do it.

And having nunchucks to hit them with (or are they numchucks?). You know, those little poles connected with a chain. You might wonder why those are better than just hitting your opponent with a full-sized baseball bat. It's because your opponent is probably thinking that you're doing some kind of little performance for him with your special sticks, so you guys are kind of friends now, and then you SUDDENLY hit him in the face and he's badly hurt — especially his feelings.

Actually, probably especially his face.

Either way, he was unprepared.

Anyway, Aunt Carol came over after dinner to borrow something of my mom's. Out of NOWHERE, she nunchucks me in the face with her words by saying the following to my dad, who is on the couch concentrating on a TV commercial.

"Hey, I heard about your friend and the plates. Pretty exciting," she says, obviously because Angeline had shared my lie with her.

My dad turns to her and makes this face like Aunt Carol had just said how much she likes the smell of **wet cats**.

"Yeah," he said slowly, and then looked at me, confused.

I shrugged.

"People love plates," I said to him. "What are you gonna do?"

It was good to know how marvelous I was at lying and how good my dad was at it, too. What a **great idea** it was to lie, I thought.

Just lie all the time.

Lie, lie, lie.

I had to eat **Fibergrunt Flakes** the next morning, and as I sat there gnawing them into a gray paste smooth enough to swallow, I thought about how much better the world would be if we all **lied**.

Like, if I worked at the factory where they made Fibergrunt Flakes, when nobody was looking, I would just dump a huge bag of sugar into the big cauldron where they were stirring it all up.

"Jamie, did you add sugar to this?" some sad cereal maker would ask me as he tasted it and found it suddenly **not as sickening**.

"Nope," I would say. "It's just good now. It just tastes good now for some unknown reason that nobody knows. It just does. Just roll with it."

And he'd be satisfied with that, and the people who bought it and ate it would finally be happy, and what's wrong with that? **What's wrong with being happy?**

I know that people say it's wrong to add things to people's food and not tell them. But guess what — **I actually talked to the people that say that**, and we had a long conversation about it, and now they say it's fine. They said that they were wrong, and it's fine now.

See? Another lie. I just lied, and it sounded great. **Works every time.**

And I was going to need the lies to work like that again.

Like, the next day.

I didn't know much about Angeline's young childhood. But it's a known fact that the school has a **PERMANENT RECORD** of everybody, and all your bad grades and terrible deeds and events of your childhood are recorded in it forever. Once, I had brief access to Angeline's permanent record, but I never read it. Later, she told me that there were terrible things in there that could have destroyed her, and I felt a deep sense of pride for not invading her privacy, and even **deeper regret** for not having a copy of those things to stick up her nose later.

Not knowing what was in there nearly drove Isabella insane, and in a carefully planned scheme in which she got herself sent to the assistant principal's office (Uncle Dan) at the exact time a bee flew into his office (he's allergic to bees, she learned), she managed to quickly pull open a file drawer and shoot a single photo of one thing in Angeline's **PERMANENT RECORD** before he managed to return to his office with Aunt Carol to kill the bee for him.

It wasn't actually a bee anyway. It was a fly that she had secretly released from a jar. I talked Isabella into using a fly because a bee could make him really sick, but mostly because it would be more **hilariously embarrassing** when Aunt Carol discovered that he had almost cried about a fly.

Later, when we looked at the photo of Angeline's record, we could see just the top of one report that said something about hitting and, in front of that, the full page of one about **SOMETHING AWFUL**. We were ~~thrilled~~ shocked to discover that it was for stealing, but our spirits fell as we read deeper.

Angeline had stolen some mints off a teacher's desk. Just a little pack of mints. It's still stealing, of course, but . . .

The **CRIME IN PROGRESS**

It was second grade. She had learned about the people who work at the sewage treatment plant that have to purify all our wastewater. She was so concerned about the smell that they had to put up with that she started flushing the mints down the toilet, one at a time, in an effort to improve things at the sewage treatment facility miles away.

This was just so, so, *SO* sickeningly adorable, that when Angeline's mom told the people at the facility about it, they presented Angeline with the title of **Water Princess**, and she was on the news.

The only reason it was in her permanent record at all was because, technically, there was a theft, and the school has to record everything like that, even **the cutest crime of the century**.

See? Angeline really does genuinely care about people. **Gross, right?**

The disgusting criminal

I've always felt that Angeline has it all. I mean, she has skin like a Barbie, hair like a Barbie, and eyelashes like, I don't know, a Barbie, I guess.

People absolutely love her on sight, and to make things worse, she's not just a pretty face. She's actually a very kind human being. Very kind. Terribly, terribly kind.

KIND. KIND. KIND.

Which is why I **kind** of hate her sometimes.

But beauty fades. It just doesn't last forever, and incredibly, there are actually people in the world who are **JEALOUS** of people with hair like golden silk and a voice like a silver flute and lips that evidently naturally salivate their own gloss. Extreme attractiveness can work against these people.

This is why I have always strived for just the right amount of attractiveness.

Anyway, Angeline, like so many of us, will have to learn to do something for a living one day.

She could be a PERFUME COW. Like where they just harvest her naturally good aroma and yes this is probably a real thing maybe

I always thought she could be a supermodel, but Angeline doesn't like being thought of as just pretty. She always wants to **do** something — to accomplish something. Just being beautiful isn't enough for her. It's probably the one thing about her that's just like me.

Why do they call them **SUPER**models anyway?

CHAPTER NINETEEN
THE COW WAS DOWN WITH IT

"We won't have to look at **these** much longer," Mom chirped as she brought our dinner in from the kitchen and set the plates down in front of us.

"That's a relief," Dad said. "**Ugliest meatballs** I've ever seen." He chuckled and looked over at me. "I'm glad she said it, and not me."

I laughed a little, too, mostly because these weren't even close to the ugliest meatballs Mom had ever made. Once, she made some with holes poked through the middle. She thought they looked like adorable little donuts, but the hole just looked like the **screaming mouth** of a meatball shrieking in horror at what it had become.

"I was talking about the plates," Mom said flatly.

Dad was chewing absently until he caught Mom's scowling stare.

"I meant the **PLATES**," she repeated. "We won't have to look at these **plates** much longer."

If you've ever sat with a large, quiet cow and described the different planets in our solar system, and how they all revolve around the sun, and how the sun is really just a star, you have a **very good idea** of what my dad looked like in that moment.

"Because you're getting her **new plates**," I said, nudging his large cow shoulder.

"New. Plates," the large, quiet cow repeated dim-wittedly.

"For your anniversary," I prompted.

"OH!" he said, really big like that. "Right. From Kathleen."

"Kirsten," I reminded him.

"Kirsten. Yup. The plates. Yup. I am. Yup."

I suddenly had the impression that this whole plate thing may have actually been Dad's very first attempt at lying. I simultaneously realized that I had said the word "PLATES" more in the last few days than ever before in my life.

The thought of saying "plates" and talking about plates and thinking about plates suddenly enraged me. I felt the anger rising up from my guts. I heard my teeth grind, and I felt my face turn hot — hot enough to warm a small lunch item.

There are only so many times in a week that you can think about plates. There are only so many times you can say the word "**PLATES.**"

Thunder cracked.

Somewhere, I mean. Probably. But if it had happened at my house right then, that would have been really perfect.

My fists came down on the table with a crash, and a meatball tumbled off the table and landed directly in between Stinker and Stinkette.

Amazingly, Stinker didn't try to eat it, so Stinkette **gobbled it up** in one piggish bite.

Mom and Dad stared at me. They didn't look angry. They looked more amazed that this **THING** was living in their house, pounding their table and launching their meatballs.

"I'm sorry," I said, which was strange because I'm usually not sorry about things, but this time I really might have been.

"Angeline is making us nuts with these paper plates of hers, and I know it's because she's really concerned about money and her future, but honestly, I don't think I ever want to hear about plates again. I think maybe I hate plates now."

And that's when it happened.

I realized that maybe **everybody** hates them.

I mean, all my favorite foods don't require them — ice-cream cones, tacos, pizza — you just pick them up and go. You don't need plates.

The world didn't need Angeline's plates. The world didn't need **any** plates. It needed to be **plateLESS**, or **plate-FREE**.

I knew exactly what I needed to do.

My favorites don't need plates!

SANDWICH!

HAMBURGER!

FROSTING!

FROSTING SANDWICH!

Four hours later, my first attempt was complete. I used a pair of pliers and some coat hangers to create it.

I called it the **Deliciousness Tree**. Here's what it looked like:

AMAZ ING!

There were eight prongs, and that seems like enough for everything I could think of.

This wasn't merely corn on the cob, it was everything on the cob. Imagine walking down the street, eating bites of this and that, without the nuisance of plates or silverware. It would be like a **Dream Come True**.

Okay, not a Dream Come True, exactly. Maybe like a **Dreamish Come Truish**. But that's still pretty good.

I showed it to Stinker, since he's pretty severely into food, but he wasn't interested. I figured that the whole plate issue was lost on him, since, as a dog, everywhere in the world is a plate to him.

I showed it to my dad, and he just reached for it and began eating, as though this was how he had always been served food.

"**Dad. Wait. Stop.** Did you notice my invention?"

His tongue was maneuvering a cube of cheese from a prong with the dexterity you normally only see in anteaters.

"It's great, sweetheart. Go get Daddy another one."

It had passed the **first** critical test. Other inventions of mine had not done so well with Dad, so this was a big win.

The Inventions That were **NOT** Dad Approved

That outfit made mostly from Mom's old bras

My space-saving vertical hammock

The STEAKNANA (MEAT packaged like a banana) ok he was kinda ok with this

But I knew I had to pass a harder test. I had to get Isabella and Angeline on board. Angeline was so obsessed with her plates, it was going to be nearly impossible for her to go along with this.

CHAPTER TWENTY
ANGELINE WON'T LIKE THIS

"I love this," Angeline said sincerely. "It's perfect for all the people who won't like our other product. You're covering all the bases, Jamie. You're so clever."

She stood there twirling the **Deliciousness Tree** as Isabella watched and puckered her lips thoughtfully.

"What do you think?" I asked her. I really needed Isabella's support on this.

"Jamie," she began, "I've seen a lot of ideas in my time — really great ideas — but honestly, I haven't cared about any of them."

"Except this one?" I asked hopefully.

"I don't have an opinion," she said. "If an idea **benefits** me, I like it. If it doesn't, I don't. Until it does one of those things or the other, I really just don't care about it."

GENUINE ADMIRATION

"Don't listen to her," Angeline said, handing it back. "This is great. We need to test it right away."

It's always hard when you get encouragement and enthusiasm from somebody who isn't the one you really wanted it from.

"We'll make a bunch of them and test them in the cafeteria, like we did with the plates," Angeline went on. "By the way, what's going on with the people who are going to make them?"

I took a long drink of my Pepsi as I thought about how to handle this.

Thinking geniusly, I dropped the **Deliciousness Tree** to the ground. When Angeline bent down to pick it up, I swiftly dabbed a blob of ketchup under my nose to appear exactly like I had a bloody nose.

"EWWWW!" Angeline gasped. "You have a bloody nose."

Isabella calmly reached across the table, wiped her finger under my nose, and stuck it **in her mouth**.

She smacked her lips.

"That's just **ketchup**," she said.

"How did you know that?" Angeline said.

"I didn't," Isabella said.

Not **exactly** what I was hoping for, but Angeline shivered, stood up in utter disgust, and walked away stiffly.

"Is there something you're not telling me?" Isabella asked, reaching for one of my French fries. "Friends don't keep things from each other."

"You keep things from me all the time," I said.

"You're right, Jamie. I do. But do you see how I openly just **admitted** that to you? See how I didn't keep that from you? That's because I'm a true friend. You can learn from me."

I asked Isabella if she'd help me make my **Deliciousness Trees,** and she said that she'd be delighted to help as long as absolutely nothing else in the whole world came up ever.

Important things that could come up.

Sock drawer requires immediate organization

Homework overdue from kindergarten must be finished

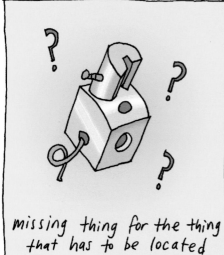

missing thing for the thing that has to be located

Sock drawer is much too organized. Must be messed up.

Surprisingly, something else in the whole world came up, and Isabella couldn't come over. But Angeline was ready to help twist up some **Deliciousness Trees.**

We had all the stuff spread out on the kitchen table when my dad walked in. He's always so warm to my friends.

"**Hi, Angela,**" he said.

"Hi, Mr. Kelly," she said, politely ignoring his error.

"Her name is **Ange*line*,**" I said.

"I know that. What did I say? I said Angeline."

"You said Ange*la*," I said.

"No, I didn't."

"Angeline," I said, "what did he call you?"

I should have known better. There was no way she was going to correct him. I brought it on myself.

"Thanks so much for helping us out with the plates," she said sweetly.

"What plates?"

"DAD, DAD, DAD. THE PLATES. YOU KNOW, THE ONES WITH KIRSTEN HALL. THOSE PLATES. NOW LEAVE US ALONE HERE. WE'RE BUSY, OKAY?"

He started to mumble.

"Why is everybody all of a sudden so dang interested in pla —"

"Dad, we're going to talk about **BRAS** now," I said, and he scurried out before he had to hear his daughter utter a single sentence with the words "**CUP SIZE**" in it.

"Dads, huh?" I said as I sat back down. "They're such a pain."

"It's not easy for dads," Angeline said softly, and I knew she was thinking of her dad, out of work and worried. I wish I could have said something encouraging, but then I realized the only thing I could have said would have been:

"Don't fret, Angeline, I've constructed a gigantic lie to trick you into feeling some false hope. Isn't that considerate of me?"

DAD FRIGHTENER

"Let's load up a couple of these things and see how they look," I said, masterfully changing the subject, and we started jamming things on the **Deliciousness Trees**. The bits that fell were quickly snapped up by Stinkette — but not Stinker, who seemed slightly less greedy and disgustingly fat than usual.

"Can I take one of these home to show my dad?" Angeline asked, and the look of concern that had been on her face for the last few days was completely washed away by her crazy blindingly beautiful smile. I normally can't stand how **naturally dazzling** she is, but for just a second, I would have let her take anything in our house to her dad.

It's like I wanted her to be happy.

Ew.

The next day in class, we showed the **Deliciousness Trees** to Mr. Henzy.

"They're made from coat hangers," I said.

"I can see that," Mr. Henzy said. "They're like some sort of clever kebabs."

"OH, JAMIƎ!" Angeline squealed. "Klever Kebabs! With a *K*! That's way better than Deliciousness Trees."

I looked at Isabella for some support.

"It's a jillion times better," she said with a shrug.

I huffed.

"I'm not sure coat hangers are safe for food," Mr. Henzy said. "Maybe there's another way to make these."

"I think coat hangers are okay. Don't you, Isabella?" I said, looking at her for support.

"They're probably not," she said. "They might have residue of detergent or dry-cleaning chemicals on them. Plus, the ends of those look pretty stabby. They could probably poke out an eye or pierce a larynx."

"What's a larynx?"

"It's in your throat," she explained. "Your voice box. You **punch** people in it."

"Thanks, Isabella."

"And I'm not sure why these kebabs with multiple prongs would be better than just a single stick anyway," Mr. Henzy said.

Isabella stood up and cleared her larynx.

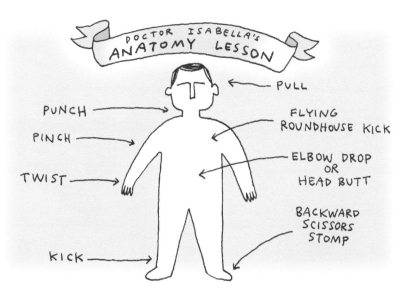

"Because, Mr. Henzy, we don't like shish kebabs telling us what order we should eat things in. **We** want to decide. And there are some things we don't want to eat at all. We don't want to have to eat a mushroom as a penalty for getting down to the piece of chicken. This is the future, old man. It's time for you to get with the times and deal with the New Kebab Reality."

She sat back down, and the entire class applauded. Calling him "**OLD MAN**" probably wasn't necessary, but Mr. Henzy started laughing and clapped a little himself.

Okay, now **THAT** was the kind of support I was looking for. Thanks, Isabella.

Mr. Henzy studied the ~~Deliciousness Tree~~ **Klever Kebab** for a moment.

"This isn't quite ready to test yet, Jamie. How about if you let me knock this around a little and see if I can find somebody to help you with it?"

Was this more of his **AWWWW-ful** faith in me again? Was he going to try to teach me something again? We both knew he couldn't do it.

It's hard to know if you should **trust** a teacher. One day, when they were children, they went to school, and they never found their way back out again as long as they lived. You can only assume that they are either very dumb because they never figured out how to escape, or very smart because they've been going to school for seventy-five years.

Angeline squealed.

"Now we can do these **AND** the plates. Jamie's dad has somebody who is going to make the plates!"

Mr. Henzy looked appropriately puzzled.

"Why? I thought your test on those failed," he said with the blunt, clear, logical thinking of somebody you wish would just shut up.

Isabella said, "He's right. They bombed. I hadn't thought of that. **Why** would anybody be interested in those plates, Jamie?"

I looked at Angeline. She just **blinked**.

(Pretty blinking sound)

"Maybe plate experts know something about plates that we don't know," I said. "Maybe they have special plate strategies or something. I mean, look around — there are plates EVERYWHERE. The plate guys are doing *something* right."

And then I put everything I had into giving them all a withering dirty look, designed to make them feel stupid for asking.

And it **worked**.

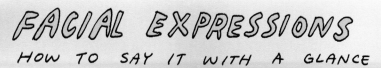

"You should not have asked me that."

"Not impressed."

"Isabella, where did you get that, and are you sure it's dead?"

"Quick, take my picture."

"Oh. You have a beagle, too?"

"Take another one."

CHAPTER TWENTY-ONE
DIRTY BOXES

Angeline never **shut up** about our big plate company. My dad, seeming to know what she was talking about, helped me stall for time, but it also amplified her commitment. I figured that the longer I stalled, the more likely it was that Angeline's dad would just get a new job and we could drop the whole dumb charade. You know, like we did with the Easter Bunny and the Tooth Fairy. (But not zombies. Dude, those are real.)

This strategy may have worked, except that Mr. Henzy was still all interested in math and teaching us Personal Finance stuff. So every time he started talking about the cost of living, I watched Angeline add up numbers, cross them out, chew her lip, and **add them up** again.

Normally, this amount of lip chewing is hard on lips, but it was just making hers look pinker and plumper. It's like that time she had one split end, and it made it look like she had **seven times** as much hair.

SHE even MADE A CASE OF PINKEYE LOOK ADORABLE

"Who can tell me how much they need to earn a year in order to cover their basic living expenses?" Mr. Henzy asked with the kind of big, broad teacher smile that assures you that they have no idea of how much you wish they'd just **stop**.

A few hands went up, including Dicky's, but teachers often ignore his hand because it's usually just a request to go wash his shoes or belt or something else that nobody but Dicky does at school.

THERE'S MORE

OH,
DICKY

Angeline didn't raise her hand, and **NOT** raising your hand is like waving a red cape in front of a bull. Teachers call on you the most when you don't want to be called on. It's like how cats know who is allergic to them, so they always choose to jump up on that person's lap.

He called on her, and she said she didn't know the answer — but she really did. She's not great at math, but this is really important to her and I know she has it all figured out now. She just didn't want to talk about it because it would make her upset.

So Mr. Henzy started throwing the real numbers at us, and it just seemed impossible. I don't know how my parents do it. I don't know how **anybody** does it.

That night at dinner, or whatever you want to call what Mom served us, I told them I couldn't believe how they managed to keep it all going — our lives, the budget, all the expenses. I said that I was totally impressed that we didn't live in a dirty box down by the lake.

They seemed to appreciate my appreciation.

"**Is** there a dirty box available?" Dad asked. "Because that does sound like it could be a bit more affordable."

OUR DIRTY BOX HOME

I'LL HAVE TO MAKE A CARDBOARD LAWN MOWER TO USE ON OUR DIRTY CARDBOARD LAWN

Dad bragged about my **Deliciousness Tree** invention to Mom and told her how it was so great that he was sure I would be able to sell it for millions of dollars and we would be able to afford our own individual dirty boxes and not have to share, and we could have one for Stinker and one for Stinkette and maybe an extra dirty old box for Isadora if I wanted to invite her for a sleepover.

I was having so much **fun** that I didn't even correct him.

Mom trying to look dignified in her dirty box ↱

Wishing I hadn't invited her ↓

Stinker somehow managing to be even grosser than his box ↗

CHAPTER TWENTY-TWO
THE SALAD

Dicky counted my chews.

"Eight, nine, ten."

I swallowed.

"Dicky, don't do that," I said. "Let me eat my salad, and don't **count my chews**."

"You should chew every bite fifty times before you swallow it," he said. "Or a hundred."

"I don't even chew my gum fifty times before I swallow it," Isabella said, and she wasn't kidding. Isabella chews a **mouthful of meat** four times at the most.

"You need to chew your food well to make *going to the restroom* easier," he whispered.

"Birds don't even have teeth," Isabella pointed out. "Doesn't seem like they're having any trouble going to the restroom. You should hear my dad swear about what they do to his car."

"Yeah, and whispering doesn't make it okay to talk about, Dicky," I said, taking a long drink of my Coke.

"I'm going to go count somebody else's chews," he said, and waddled away.

"Where's Angeline?" Isabella asked. "Why isn't she here bugging you about your dad and the plate company?"

"I have no idea." I took another huge bite of salad and tried to talk as I chewed it. "But I need to tell you something, and you have to promise not to tell Angeline."

Isabella smiled weirdly.

"I promise," she said.

"It's about the plates."

She nodded.

"That woman isn't going to make them," I said.

"Bummer," Isabella said. "Maybe we can change them somehow . . . you know, make something that the woman will make."

"There is no woman making the plates," I confessed. "I made it all up."

I looked into Isabella's eyes, expecting some sort of judgment, but I saw none. She wasn't even looking at me. She was looking at something just over my head — and she was shaking her head **no**.

She was looking at **Angeline**.

Angeline reached down and grabbed my Coke. She looked me right in the eyes, with a combination of anger and hurt feelings on her face, and slowly poured the Coke **all over my salad**.

Then she opened her hand and let the empty can fall on the floor. She walked away quickly.

"Angeline, wait!" I said, running after her. "I was trying to make you feel better."

"Funny how rarely lying to your friends makes them feel better," she said coldly. Really coldly. **Really, really coldly.** Colder than a baby bunny with the flu lost in the middle of a snowstorm in the dead of night with one sock wearing a soaking wet sweater listening to wolves howling a hundred yards away.

You just don't know what to say to a bunny like that. I walked back to the lunch table.

Where Isabella had **finished** my salad.

CHAPTER TWENTY–THREE
HARD TO WASH OFF

"You ate my salad?"

"It was **good** with the Coke dumped on it," Isabella said.

"There was dressing on it, too," I said.

"I don't know what to tell you." She shrugged. "It wasn't bad. Somehow it tasted less like a plate of **assorted garbage** than most salads do."

I had to wonder what was going on inside Isabella's body at that exact moment when it was faced with plants for the **very first time**.

I spent the rest of that week trying to talk to Angeline. She was really, really mad at me.

I knew this because when Angeline is really, really mad at you, she sends you a letter on really pretty stationery to let you know. The envelope had stickers on it, sure, but I could tell that they were the **worst stickers** on the whole sheet of stickers.

Empty Ice cream cone

Burnt Brussels Sprout

Little Seeds

small dish with hair in it

Rash

It read:

Dear Jamie,

We've been friends for a very long time, and I even feel like we're family since your Aunt Carol married my Uncle Dan. It's difficult for me to understand why you would be so insensitive to me at a time when I really needed my friends the most.

I'm very sorry to inform you that your services as a friend are no longer required, and I'll thank you for not contacting me again in any way.

Very truly yours,
Angeline

P.S. The word I used at the end there is "truly," and it refers to something called the truth. I know the word is unfamiliar to you. It means "sincerity, honesty, or accuracy." As in the sentence "The girl was truly hurt when the gross warthog-person lied to her."

And on top of that it, the letter was **unscented**. **EVERYTHING** of Angeline's smells good. The fact that this letter was unscented meant that she took the time to actually **wash the perfumey fragrance off of it**. It probably took her a half hour.

Angeline stayed mad.

For weeks, I tried everything I could think of to bring her around.

I decorated her locker with **spectacular glittery wonderfulness.** But one slash, and it fell to the ground in shreds. Those nails of hers are as sharp as they are gorgeous.

I started working extra hard on the **recycling** at our house and sent her pictures of me doing it — rinsing things out, separating the different materials, all that stuff. Angeline is big on recycling, and I thought she'd approve. Isabella never recycles. She says she won't wash her garbage.

I even started a fund to help supply **guide dogs** to the older **guide dogs** who had lost their vision in the line of duty, but still wanted to help their blind masters. I realize now that this probably isn't a real thing, but it seemed like a good idea at the time, and I liked the poster I came up with.

Nothing worked.

Isabella was over one day after school so that we could **not** study together. (It's a thing we do.) She sat on my bed with her feet up on Stinker. She knew I was still trying to apologize to Angeline.

"I'm glad she's not bugging us about those dumb plates anymore," she said. "You should be glad, too. How many more of those fake things did you want to make, anyway? And why do you even care what Angeline thinks? Since when are we really friends with her?"

I couldn't answer that. Sometimes friendships **grow** — like flowers, or stuff in the shower drain.

"What do I have to do to make it up to her?" I shouted, as if shouting might help.

"Get her dad his job back," Isabella said.

I knew that she was right, and that it was impossible for me to do.

I reached under my bed and grabbed the stack of plates I had made. I had drawn the designs, but Angeline had given me all the calorie and nutritional information. I had to admit, she knew **a lot** about food.

"How about if you and I go downstairs and make something for me to eat?" Isabella suggested as she slid off my bed, dragging the sheets and blankets onto the floor.

Stinkette jumped up on me and barked. The word "EAT" was all she needed to hear. Both she and Stinker have a large vocabulary of food-related words . . . and very few others.

Stinker didn't move at all. He must have already eaten a pair of my rubber boots or something, and wouldn't be ready for another snack for an hour or so.

WORDS BEAGLES KNOW	WORDS BEAGLES DO NOT KNOW
EAT	SIT
FOOD	SHUT UP
NOM	SERIOUSLY STOP BARKING
SNACK	BE QUIET
APPETIZER	BE QUIET
DINNER	STOP
SUPPER	STOP IT
DESSERT	

Downstairs, Mom was getting dinner ready when we walked into the kitchen.

"No snacks," she said. "I don't want you to spoil your appetites."

"That's your job," I whispered under my breath.

"Isabella can stay for dinner if it's okay with her folks."

"It's okay," Isabella said.

"Don't you have to call them?"

"Nope. It's easier on everybody when I'm not there. Or when my brothers aren't. Or when my parents aren't. Actually, I'll bet the best dinner we ever had together was when **none of us** were there."

My mom didn't question it. Long ago, she came to the understanding that Isabella's family isn't really a huggy-kissy kind of family. Accepting a hug means that the person is close enough to choke you, and a kiss is just two lips away from a bite.

She ALSO BeLieves that HOLDING HANDS MIGHT JUST Be A TRICK TO JUDO THROW you

HYAH

We sat down for dinner and waited patiently for Mom to bring it in from the kitchen. I'm always willing to help, but Mom likes to be in charge of the presentation. It's like that thrilling moment just before Dracula leaps out and bites you.

I hate Mom's cooking less when Isabella is over because it's fun to watch Isabella try to **guess** what is.

Dad sat down and nodded at us.

"Hey, Jamie. Hey, Isadora."

"Hi, Mr. Gardenhose," Isabella said without flinching.

"Dad," I barked. "It's Isa*bella*. Why do you get it wrong every time?"

"Well, she got my name wrong."

"She only does that when you do it to her first."

COULD BE PANCAKE
COULD BE BURNT
UNDERPANTS

Mom brought in dinner, and Isabella actually made a little gasping sound. Mom thought it was because she was impressed, but it was really because she was startled by how **severely saladish** the dinner was.

It was a giant chef's salad. It had lots of meat and cheese, but also lots of vegetables.

And then there was a knock at the door, followed by my Aunt Carol's voice as she let herself in.

"Hello! Hope we aren't interrupting," she sang. "We're on our way to the movies, and I thought we'd stop by and see if anybody wanted to join us."

Angeline followed Aunt Carol around the corner and eyed me scornfully. It was clear that this visit was **NOT** her idea. She wouldn't have even come in, except that her good manners are more powerful than her hate, and waiting in the car would have been rude.

"If you can wait until they finish eating, I bet Jamie and Isabella will go," Mom said. "Will you join us? I'll get you some plates."

Isabella stood up and walked into the kitchen, presumably to help my mom.

"*Plates*," Angeline hissed.

"I know, right?" Dad said as he chewed. "I'm with you, Angela. Enough already."

"No, thanks. We already ate," Aunt Carol said.

"Plates," Angeline repeated.

"What was that?" My mom asked her.

"**NOTHING,**" I said loudly, but Angeline seemed to be on a tattletale mission. I knew I was going to be in trouble in a minute.

I bent down under the table and smacked myself in the nose. Nobody could be mad at me if I was bleeding, right?

It didn't work. **My nose wouldn't bleed.**

Who knew
I had an
INDESTRUCTIBLE
nose?

"I said *plates*, Mrs. Kelly," Angeline said. "Jamie, Isabella, and I were working on a plate project. I really had high hopes for it."

Isabella piped up as she returned from the kitchen. "Right. Because her dad got fired and now they're broke and Angeline can't go to college and will probably end up poor and maybe miserable."

I sprayed bits of salad when I yelled.

"ISABELLA!"

"She's right," Angeline said. "Isabella's telling the truth. And my plate idea was dumb. I know that now. But Jamie lied to me. She said that somebody named Kirsten Hall was interested in helping with the plates. Remember? Even you told me that, Mr. Kelly. Why did you lie to me, too?"

"Yeah, Dad," I said, skillfully trying to deflect the blame. "You made up that whole thing about getting Mom new plates. You're a bigger liar than me when you think about it because, you know, you're bigger. By at least a hundred pounds."

"Wait! I did get her new plates!" Dad said. "The saleslady had to order them. Her name was Kirsten Hall." Dad left the room and came back with a receipt.

Mom read the receipt. "This says **Katherine Hess**."

"Right. Katherine Hess. That's what I said."

"Hang on," I protested. "If you're telling the truth, where are these new plates?"

Isabella held up her **TOTALLY** empty plate. She was the only one who had finished her salad. It dripped with the remains of the Coke she had poured over it while we were arguing.

"Iff thif ff?" she said through a mouthful of lettuce.

"Yes!" Dad said. "See? Brand-new plates. Just like I said. From **Katharine Hepburn.**"

It *was* a new plate. I moved some of my salad heap aside. I hadn't noticed the plates before. I had to admit, they were lovely.

"Isabella, did you pour a Coke on that salad?" my mom asked.

Isabella dragged her sleeve across her mouth and grinned. "Yup."

"Isabella! **You can't do that!** You can't put Coke on a salad. Think of the calories!"

"Two tablespoons of ranch dressing has a hundred and fifty calories," Angeline said without hesitating. "An entire can of Coke has a hundred and forty. The dressing has at least five times as much sodium. I'm not saying it's a good idea, but in lots of ways, it's no worse."

"Go get me a Coke," Dad told me . . . but Mom shook her head.

"Plus, she *did* eat the whole salad," Angeline said. "So at least she got vitamins A, C, and K, plus potassium, folate, and some fiber. It's not ideal, but I've never seen her eat anything with a leaf on it before. It's a start."

I had to give Angeline credit. That cupcake knows a ton about food, and I couldn't help smiling at her — a real, authentic, **I'm-So-Impressed-With-You Smile**. Angeline wanted to stay mad, but she could see the sincerity in my eyes.

I mean, how the heck did she know so much about food like that? And right off the top of her ~~hair~~ head?

Dad took another bite of his salad and suddenly stopped chewing. "Angelo got fired?"

"Who's Angelo?" I asked him.

"My dad," Angeline said quietly.

"His name is **Angelo**?" I asked.

She nodded.

THIS name my dad gets right.

He doesn't know these:

Isabella

Angeline

me

All the rest

The next day, Angeline still sat at a different table at lunch.

I figured that the United States and England must have had a time, sometime after the Revolutionary War, when they sat down at a **lunch table** together.

And George Washington would have, like, made eye contact with The King of England.

And The King would be all like, "Hey. I saw they put you on the dollar bill or whatever."

And George Washington would have been all like, "Oh yeah. They didn't even tell me they were doing that. I would have done something about my **weird hair.**"

And The King of England would have laughed and said, "It **was** kind of weird."

But George Washington would have been okay with that and known it wasn't really an insult, and they would have just eaten their lunches and not had another war or anything.

Angeline and I have to be **AT LEAST** as smart as those guys.

So I got up and sat at her table.

I made eye contact, just like George Washington probably did.

"Get lost," Angeline said, just like how The King of England didn't.

I took a deep breath. "Angeline, I lied to you to try to make you feel better. I lied to you because I hated how sad you were. I lied to you because you're my friend."

"That does make me feel better," Angeline said. "But how do I know that you're not just lying **NOW** to make me feel better? **YOU DO THAT**, you know. You just said so."

Isabella sat down next to me with a salad.

"Give me your Coke," she said.

"I don't have one. I have a Sprite today." I handed it over, and she dumped it all over her salad. Mike Pinsetti, who was walking past, stopped to watch Isabella drown her lunch in soda pop.

"Look, Angeline," I said, "I've been trying to apologize for weeks now. Would I have recycled all that stuff if I wasn't sincere?"

"You should be recycling anyway."

"Would I have tried to set up that dumb guide dog thing?"

"**You're dumb**, Jamie. Nobody notices when you do one more additional dumb thing."

I know, right? Angeline called me **dumb**. Angeline has to be pretty angry to be as mean as I am on a regular basis.

Refuse to whistle while she works.

Won't just turn that frown upside down

Will hardly even sing to the woodland creatures that come every morning to help her get dressed.

spits a little

I leaned in close and spoke quietly.

"I know this thing with your dad has you worried. Personally, I blame Mr. Henzy for making us learn how much things cost. I mean, when you think about it, it's **all his fault.** You with me?" I put up my hand for a high five that never came.

"I know that you feel like you need to start saving for college, and you thought your plate thing might be one of those million-dollar ideas that would take care of it for you. I saw how worried you were, and I wanted to cheer you up. But I know I shouldn't have lied to you. I should have just —"

That's when I realized that Angeline wasn't looking at me. She was looking at something **over my shoulder.**

Isabella had drawn a little crowd. Pinsetti had sat down next to her and poured Sprite all over his salad, too.

Other kids were asking questions and reaching in for a sample. They were nodding in approval.

"Jamie," Angeline said, her voice trembling. **"Jamie. This. This. This."**

Her soft hands clutched my arm, and her fingernails dug in as the aloe in her hand lotion soothed the cuts as she was inflicting them.

CHAPTER TWENTY-FOUR
MORE EXCITEMENT

Angeline had come back to life.

She believed that **this** was the idea that was going to work. As excited as she was about the HEALTH-O-PLATES, she was a jillion times more excited about this salad thing.

I realized that Angeline is an expert on being excited.

The next day, we gathered in my kitchen with cans of Coke and Pepsi and root beer and cream soda and lettuce.

Isabella sat there watching over us, using her special gift: being an expert at **hating things**. She can hate things the rest of us never even thought of hating. This made her especially well qualified for the job of sampling our salad dressing concoctions and deciding whether she hated them or not.

She also HATES

parallel bacon

WHATEVS

spiders that aren't trying

artificial mustache fragrance

Flavors are a lot like colors and textures. I'm an expert at combining things like this in order to make gross things fabulous or delicious. I've spent my whole life trying to turn my mom's cooking into something I **could eat**.

As a team, we were bizarrely qualified, like a **mythological hero** who was made of three people.

We came up with **a lot** of salad dressings.

We discovered that adding salt is important, as well as some kind of herb. Garlic worked pretty well. And parsley, even though I'm not sure I could taste the individual ingredients after they were mixed together. It was like people in a crowd yelling — you can't really tell what any one person is saying.

We tried adding lemon or lime here and there, and Mom showed us how to boil something for a while to make it thicker. Mom learned this trick once when she boiled something too long, which was pretty much **every single time** she ever boiled something.

Also, adding cornstarch will thicken stuff up, but you have to mix it into cold water first because if you just dump it right into the boiling stuff you get horrible wads and clumps. Looking back, I think that Mom also learned this trick on those occasions when she served us **Wads 'n' Clumps** for dinner.

Isabella had figured out a way to quickly taste the dressings and let us know her expert hateful opinions. She would dip a small piece of lettuce into each sample and either:

A) Swallow it

or

B) Discharge it from her mouth like a cannon.

The salad dressings that she didn't spray all over the table were the ones we set aside, planning adjustments to make them even better.

Isabella invented
THE
GLORIOUS
RAINBOW
OF
HATRED

But then Isabella tried **dressing number forty-two**. It was dark brown, a little thick, and a little sticky.

She dipped her lettuce leaf and took a bite, and Angeline and I instinctively raised our aprons to protect our faces in case she spewed it at us the way she had twenty-three times before.

But she didn't.

She swallowed it.

And she **smiled**.

"Ladies," she said as she took another bite, "I'm very happy to say that if you tell anybody else what is in this recipe, they will find you floating facedown in the river."

It was the **sweetest** thing she could have said.

I mean that. This really is the sweetest thing Isabella can say.

Somehow this is a compliment

There are advantages when your uncle is the assistant principal. Occasionally, you can talk him into things, like testing your salad dressing formula on a large population of human children.

We mixed up a big batch, and he let us offer it at lunch in spite of the very real possibility that it was not in any way healthy and may have had some **dog hair** in it.

We didn't put any dog hair in there, of course, but when you have a couple of dogs, everything you own has dog hair on it. There are **very few things** you can do about it.

Honestly all you can do is try to keep it combed

Of course the stuff was a huge hit, even with Dicky, who never gets caffeine at home. It made all the saliva **vibrate out of his mouth**, but he loved it.

Bruntford said that she thought it was a terrible idea to use soda pop as the base for a salad dressing, but Angeline carefully explained all of the calorie and fat numbers to her, and pointed out how the kids were actually finishing their salads for once, so Bruntford backed off. **(Also, Isabella kicked her.)**

We were **NOT** expecting the arrival of the news team that Aunt Carol called. They asked us questions and filmed all the kids eating. It aired on TV that night, and people started posting it online, and before you knew it, we were getting emails. **LOTS** of emails.

Everybody wanted to know the recipe. And we remembered Isabella's suggestion/threat about not revealing it.

"We're going to bottle this garbage and sell it," she said.

We looked into what that would take, and it seemed like more than we could do by ourselves.

But then we got an email from a food manufacturer that had seen the news story. They wanted to **BUY** the recipe from us.

My dad said we needed a lawyer, but Angeline and I felt that since we had Isabella, we wouldn't need a lawyer. Or a team of bodyguards.

"Are you sure you can do this, Isadora?" Dad asked her.

She lifted her foot to stomp his, but I stopped her. "Dad. **This is who she is.**"

Isabella looked into my dad's eyes, and I'm pretty sure I heard the cream in his coffee curdle. He never questioned her again.

Even Medusa doesn't want to look into her eyes

We talked about the terms of the deal, and here's how it works: We get 10% of whatever they sell it for. (They started by offering us 4%, Isabella scared them up to 8%, and then Angeline started crying, which got them up to 10% and one of their guys ran out to get her ice cream.)

Isabella also demanded that we got to name the dressing, and that our photo would be on every bottle.

We had to sign an agreement saying that we would **never** reveal the recipe to anybody else.

And then we got the check.

Isabella made them pay us an advance based on what they planned to sell in the first year. I asked how she knew how to do all this stuff, and she said that she had learned it by watching movies.

It was the biggest check I had ever seen. It was the biggest check I had ever heard of.

It's not like it will cover our college educations or anything, or buy us all hot cars or houses, but it was a great start. Plus, it was enough to convince Angeline that she was going to be able to eventually save enough, and it made her cry so hard that Isabella gave her back her ice cream.

A few days later, they arranged for us to have our picture taken for the label. They had people do our hair and makeup, and we all looked even more fabulous than usual.

They moved us into position in our matching aprons and got the lighting just right, and we all smiled these huge, beautiful grins.

A couple people screamed.

PROFESSIONAL PHOTOGRAPHER!

PROFESSIONAL MAKEUP!

DELUXE HAIRSPRAY

PROFESSIONAL APRONS!

I looked down and saw **blood** on the front of my apron. I had sprung a massive nosebleed. It seriously looked like I had inhaled a couple of tiny chainsaws.

NOW a nosebleed? Really, nose?

While Isabella tried to help me stop it, they kept photographing Angeline.

"We can Photoshop you all together on the label later," the photographer said.

Isabella and I sat there, watching Angeline beam and glow and flutter and flirt, and it was clear what we needed to do.

"The more bottles we sell, the more money we make," Isabella said quietly.

"I know. It should be Angeline on the label. **Just Angeline**," I said, crumpling a Kleenex in my fist. "She's so pretty it actually hurts my feelings."

Isabella is better at starting nosebleeds than stopping them

Angeline fought us, of course. To humor her, we took a few pictures just to show her why we felt the way we did. Next to Angeline, Isabella and I resembled **unappealing tiny older men.**

It's not something we wanted to admit, but in a way, we had accomplished our dream of **bottling and selling** Angeline.

There's a chance that Angeline is some kind of THIRD GENDER OF HYPERFEMALE.

When it came to naming the dressing, I took the lead. Angeline's face was on the label, so I wanted to make sure that Isabella and I were represented somehow. I combined our names into something catchy.

"How do you guys like *Isabelly Kelly's Salad Glamorizer*?"

Isabella gave me a thumbs-up, but Angeline knocked me over with a single high-volume squeal of delight.

"**It rhymes!**" she shrieked. "That's the best!"

There are some people you just can't say cute things to.

We had a big party at my house to unveil the name and the dressing label. The company generously sent us a big poster of the label after Isabella yelled at them to do it.

We served salads, of course, and I dared Isabella to eat broccoli, which she did — with Salad Glamorizer on it. She said the dressing was so delicious she would eat a **Band-Aid** dipped in it.

I let her try it on some Fibergrunt Flakes, but we learned that while it might work on a Band-Aid, there are things that even our Salad Glamorizer couldn't fix.

Our dads talked for a long time, which was **weird** to see. Are they somehow like us? What did they talk about?

DAD TALK!

Does this wrench go with this tie?

Do my big Dad-Jeans make my big Dad-Butt look big?

What's your favorite part of the massive sandwich that you OINK down in, like, ONE BITE?

CRAM

NOM

Do you like to lie awake at night and listen to your whiskers grow?

Hey wouldn't it be great to just sit here and not talk about stuff?

Stinkette was begging for treats all night, but Stinker was off hiding someplace. I figured it was because he didn't want to deal with a big loud crowd of people.

But I was wrong.

He was upstairs in my room.

Dead.

I couldn't remember a time when I **didn't** have Stinker. He was horrible, of course, and loud and stinky, but I loved him. He was exactly like one of my own burps.

It was Stinkette who found him, and she started whining and barking. When I came to see what was wrong, I found him, and he was **dead**.

I started screaming for Mom and Dad, and I scooped up his enormously fat body and ran out of my room and around the corner and then I accidentally **dropped him down the stairs.**

Dad was running for the kitchen and didn't see Stinker at the bottom of the stairs, and he **stepped on him**, which made this long, noisy fart sound come out of Stinker's mouth like he was a whoopee cushion.

"What is it?" Mom screamed as she followed behind Dad and also **stepped on Stinker.**

"Stop stepping on him!" I cried. **"He's dead!"**

Dad picked him up, and we all jumped in the car.

"Go to the dog hospital!" I cried, and Dad took off so fast that Stinker rolled off my lap **onto the floor.**

"Right!" Dad said, and looked at Mom. **"Where is that?"**

Mom called the vet, and she met us at her office. It was after hours, but she loves dogs in spite of having met Stinker.

Dad dropped Stinker two more times on the way from the car, and then lifted him up onto the examination table, where Stinker growled.

"He's alive!" I yelled, which startled Stinker and made him bite Dad.

We explained what had happened, and the doctor guessed that the drops and stepping-upons may have restarted Stinker's breathing, like a series of really careless and abusive Heimlich maneuvers. Dad and I congratulated ourselves on how brilliantly we had practiced medicine, and Dad proposed that stepping on a dog be called the **Kelly maneuver**.

I think partial credit for the STOMPING technique should go to Isabella

She's practically a NATURAL VETERINARIAN

After a couple of X-rays, the vet told us that Stinker had some sort of obstruction in his intestines. It was probably something he ate, but it was now causing an infection. He was in really bad shape. I suddenly realized why he hadn't been his normal greedy self for so long.

Mom and Dad said that the most humane thing to do would probably be to let the doctor put him to sleep, which is the way they say **"kill your dog"** when they know you're already upset.

"Can't they **operate** on him or something?" I said, wiping the tears off my face.

"Stinker's old," Dad said. "There's a chance he wouldn't make it. And operations like this are really expensive."

I remembered how Isabella told me that when your parents get old, you should be able to throw them out of the house, and how that seemed mean to me. And if I wouldn't do that to my parents, I wouldn't do it to an **old beagle**, either.

"I can afford it," I said. "I can pay for it — with my salad dressing money."

We discussed it for a while, and then talked it over with the vet. Mom and Dad didn't want me to spend the money, but they agreed to let me do what I wanted, so Stinker went in for an **emergency operation**. I texted Angeline and Isabella to tell them the news. They both offered to help pay for the operation with their portion of the Salad Glamorizer money, except for Isabella, but I wouldn't let them.

Stinker wasn't their problem. **He was my responsibility.**

He's like my BABY. My stinky, fat, ugly, stinky, dirty, slobbery, stinky, terrible Baby.

Afterward, the vet told us that she hadn't been sure that Stinker was going to make it, but she believed that his desire to bite more people probably **saved his life.**

Dog operations aren't covered by insurance, and I had to spend just about **everything** I had earned. I was sad about that, but I was glad that Stinker was going to be okay.

Then the doctor handed me a little bag and asked if I recognized it. It was my grandma's **bracelet** — the fancy one, the one my parents lost when they were packing up her things. Evidently, at some point, they dropped it on the floor, and Stinker ate it. That's what had messed up his guts. It was still in perfect condition, and Mom said we could sell it and maybe it would pay for the whole operation. That meant I had salad money in my bank account again.

It was touching that even though my grandma had passed away, she was still taking care of me from up in heaven. Of course, she also tried to **kill my dog** from heaven, so I suppose she has that to answer for now. **Good luck with that, Grandma.**

I got really excited when I told Dad about the bracelet. Sudden bursts of excitement bother Stinker, so he **bit** me a little, which made me try to get him to eat the bracelet again, but he wouldn't do it.

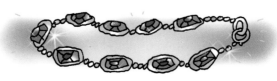

In the weeks that followed, the food company started advertising our **Salad Glamorizer**, and they told us it seemed to be selling well.

Uncle Dan said that he didn't think it was a good idea to make salads with soda pop, but he admitted that — as a person who works with kids every day — sometimes you choose the **little wrong things** over the **big wrong things**. The kids were eating more salads than ever before, and that was a pretty big deal.

Stinker recovered completely and started stealing food from his dogdaughter, Stinkette, again.

You never really know how much you **love** something until you **almost lose** it.

You also never really know how much you wish it had stayed lost until you get it back again, but for now, I'm glad Stinker is still around.

I even made him a nice card!

I LOVE YOU AND I'M SO GLAD YOU'RE OK

HEY MAYBE YOU SHOULD DIE MORE OFTEN

Love
Jamie

My dad helped Angeline's dad find a job. Apparently, he called her dad right after he heard the news, and started talking to people he knew, and just kept at it until something came up. It's not like they're close friends or anything, but he did it for Angeline — **and me**.

Now Angeline is her old self again, **inflicting delight** on everyone she sees. We've all made some progress in our bank accounts, and we owe it all to the dumbest idea we ever had: Salad Glamorizer. Even though we didn't exactly have the idea — **it just showed up**.

Mr. Henzy could not have been more proud of us. We got so much extra credit that Isabella is actually up to a low C now.

He asked us to stay after class one day just so he could tell us so.

"I'm so proud of you," he said, repeating what I wrote up there a second ago. "You young women are the next generation of inventors and businesspeople."

"Thanks," I said.

"Can we go now?" Isabella asked.

He took a box from his desk and opened it. He pulled out a neat little plastic tree and twirled it around.

"You know what this is?" he asked.

"A back scratcher?" Isabella said. In a way, she was right: She scratches her back with everything.

"It's your **Klever Kebab**," Mr. Henzy explained. "I redesigned it a bit and found a partner to make a prototype on a 3-D printer. We made it flat, so they would be easier to produce and ship. That will also cut down on the costs."

"**Great. Pay us,**" Isabella said, showing how well she had mastered the whole business-world thing.

"Of course!" Mr. Henzy said. "In fact, I'd like to have these manufactured and pay you girls a royalty, like the deal you got for your salad dressing. You're beginning quite an empire."

"You're going to quit teaching?" I asked him, optimistic that he could finally **escape** school.

"If it became the biggest product in the world, sure, I might quit. But things like this take a long time to succeed. And remember what I told you: Most of them fail. But won't it be fun to try?"

He was right. Trying is the fun part. And **why not** let him try? I'd like to help a teacher escape. If he managed to get out, other teachers would probably write a **folk song** about me.

But Angeline had an idea of her own.

Remember? Angeline Cares About People. She really, sincerely wanted to help people with her **HEALTH-O-PLATES**. She wanted to make money, too, but helping people is **REALLY** important to her — and let's face it, we're not helping people much by putting soda pop on their salads.

So we let Angeline have her way.

OKay...

So it's NOT the Best thing you could do...

Isabella made Mr. Henzy pay us an advance. She explained that he could get a business loan from a bank, just like he had taught us.

It wasn't a lot of money, but it was enough for Angeline to start the best-financed club ever at Mackerel Middle School. She bought a computer and a printer, and talked Mr. Henzy into being the supervisor.

She called it the **Kash Klub**, spelled badly in honor of the Klever Kebab, and she made it a place where kids could get information about making their ideas happen. REAL ideas, like dumb plates, and dumb salad dressing, and dumb kebabs.

She was really getting to **help** people.

Goodness pours from her like saliva from an unconscious Beagle.

Isabella was not 100% in favor of all this, obviously, since it did not meet her requirement of benefiting her.

But Angeline explained that any one of these kids could invent the next computer, or electric car, or time-travel machine, and since we'd helped them, they'd naturally want to pay us back one day.

"Blackmail," Isabella said slowly. "I like that. I'm in."

It wasn't anything like blackmail, of course, but when Isabella is happy, sometimes it's best to just go with it.

Future Isabella cashing in.

So far, none of the other kids' ideas look that great, but neither did ours when we started. Ideas often need a little time to cool off before you can tell the good dumb ones from the bad dumb ones. **After all, dumbness is a dish best served cold.**

FLYING ROBOT UNICORN

FULL FACE GLASSES

HER NAME IS ISABELLA

REMEMBERING HAT FOR DADS

So, what was **THE BIG WEIRD THING** I was talking about, Dumb Diary?

Do you think it was the success we had? Or realizing how much Angeline's happiness meant to me? Or Stinker coming back to life? Or Isabella passing math?

Those were weird things, but not the weirdest.

The Big Weird Thing is us.

Because I've realized that it won't be long before we're all going to college or starting jobs and becoming the sort of creatures that buy houses and boring cars and get all excited over new plates.

It's going to happen to us. It's going to happen to all of us.

And if there's anything **ANYWHERE** weirder than that, Dumb Diary, I'd sure like to know what it is.

Thanks for listening,

Jamie Kelly

P.S. The file.

Angeline's permanent record.

Somehow or another, Isabella let it slip that we knew about her toilet mints, and Angeline asked if we also knew about the fight. We said that we had glimpsed the file but didn't know the details.

She told us that she went through a chubby phase when she was younger, and one day, a young Mike Pinsetti called her a mean name and she **hit him** so hard she gave him a bloody nose. This explains why Mike has always been a little bit afraid of Angeline.

She got in a lot of trouble for it, but instead of letting it destroy her, she started reading the nutritional labels on packages and learning about food. That's why this cupcake knows so much about those cupcakes.

Can you guess what Mike called her to start this whole mess? **A Big Weird Thing.**

WHIP UP SOME SALAD GLAMORIZER!

Just like Jamie, Angeline, and Isabella, you can mix different ingredients to make your own salad dressing.

Try some combinations of the ingredients on the next page! (Make sure to avoid anything you're allergic to, and have an adult help, especially if you need to use the stove or a knife.)

- Garlic
- Soda pop of your choice
- Ginger
- Vinegar
- Olive oil
- Salt & pepper
- Soy sauce
- Dill
- Honey
- Basil

- Mustard
- Parsley
- Pesto
- Sugar
- Lemon juice
- Parmesan cheese
- Apple juice
- Shallots
- Cilantro
- Mint
- Maple syrup

Once you find a perfect fit, DON'T tell anyone the recipe — just enjoy your glamorous salad!

MAKE YOUR OWN HEALTH-O-PLATE!

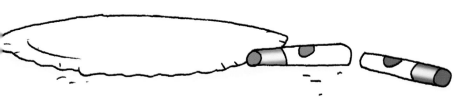

Okay, so maybe it's not a million-dollar idea, but you can still make your own fabulous Health-O-Plate to use at home.

You'll need:
- Paper plate
- Non-toxic markers

1.) Draw a line down the center of your plate.
2.) Turn the plate 90 degrees and draw another line, this time about 1/3 of the way down from the top of the plate. Now you have four sections on your plate!
3.) In the two smaller sections, write "Fruit" and "Protein." In the two larger sections, write "Vegetables" and "Grains."
4.) Decorate the outer edge of your plate however you like!

Now be like Dicky Flartsnutt and eat **everything** on your plate!

Don't miss where it all started —
Jamie Kelly's very first diary!
Be sure to look for

Turn the page for a peek . . . but whatever you do,
DON'T tell Jamie!

Wednesday 04

Dear Dumb Diary,

    Today Hudson Rivers (eighth cutest guy in my grade) talked to me in the hall. Normally, this would have no effect on me at all, since there is still a chance that Cute Guys One Through Seven might actually talk to me one day. But when Hudson said, "Hey," today, I could tell that he was totally in love with me, and I felt that I had an obligation to be irresistible for his benefit.

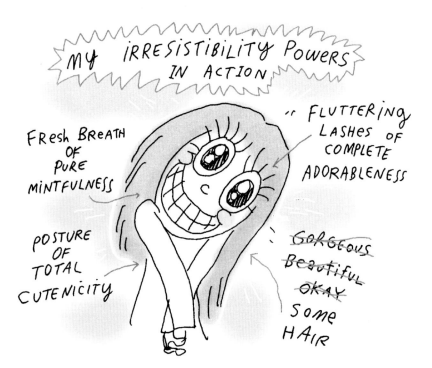

So just as I'm about to say something cool back to Hudson (Maybe even something REALLY cool. We'll never know for sure now.), Angeline comes around the corner with her jillion cute things dangling from her backpack, and intentionally looks cute RIGHT IN FRONT OF HIS EYES. This scorpion-like behavior on her part made me forget what I was going to say, so the only thing that came out of my mouth was a gush of air without any words in it. Not like this mattered, because he was staring at Angeline the same way Stinker was staring at the ball a couple days ago.

STINKER   HUDSON

It was pretty obvious that all of his love for me was squirting out his ears all over the floor. Ask Isabella if you don't believe me. She was standing right there.

As if that wasn't vicious enough, get this:

He says to Angeline: "Wow, is that your Lip Smacker I smell? ChocoMint? It's great."

Angeline stops for just a second and **LOOKS RIGHT AT ISABELLA AND ME.** Then she says to Hudson, "Yeah, it is." And her radiant smile freezes him in his tracks.

Frankly, I think that it is just rude and obscene to have teeth white enough to hurt and maybe **PERMANENTLY DAMAGE** the eyes of onlookers.

DEAR DUMB DIARY,

CAN'T GET ENOUGH JAMIE KELLY?
CHECK OUT ALL OF HER
DEAR DUMB DIARY BOOKS!

#1: Let's Pretend This Never Happened

#2: My Pants Are Haunted!

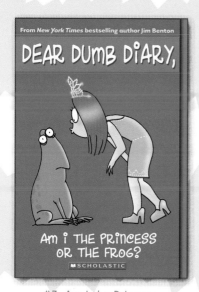

#3: Am I the Princess
or the Frog?

#4: Never Do Anything,
Ever

#5: Can Adults Become
Human?

#6: The Problem With Here Is
That It's Where I'm From

#7: Never Underestimate
Your Dumbness

#8: It's Not My Fault I Know
Everything

#9: That's What Friends
<u>Aren't</u> For

#10: The Worst Things in Life
Are Also Free

#11: Okay, So Maybe I Do
Have Superpowers

#12: Me! (Just Like You,
Only Better)

YEAR TWO #1: School. Hasn't
This Gone On Long Enough?

YEAR TWO #2: The Super-Nice
Are Super-Annoying

YEAR TWO #3: Nobody's Perfect.
I'm As Close As It Gets.

YEAR TWO #4: What I Don't
Know Might Hurt Me

YEAR TWO #5: You Can
Bet On That

YEAR TWO #6: Live Each Day
to the Dumbest

WWW.SCHOLASTIC.COM/DEARDUMBDIARY

About Jim Benton

Jim Benton is not a middle-school girl, but do not hold that against him. He has managed to make a living out of being funny, anyway.

He is the creator of many licensed properties, some for big kids, some for little kids, and some for grown-ups who, frankly, are probably behaving like little kids.

You may already know his properties: It's Happy Bunny™ or Catwad™, and of course you already know about Dear Dumb Diary.

He's created a kids' TV series, designed clothing, and written books.

Jim Benton lives in Michigan with his spectacular wife and kids. They do not have a dog, and they especially do not have a vengeful beagle.

Jamie Kelly has no idea that Jim Benton, or you, or anybody is reading her diaries. So, please, please, please don't tell her.